From North

OUR BOOKS CAN

http://north-stared.w   ...eaitions

Pierre Loti
(1850-1923)

———

MADAME
CHRYSANTHÈME
1888

———

With a Preface by ALBERT SOREL

of the French Academy

PARIS

———

About the Author.

LOUIS-MARIE-JULIEN VIAUD, "Pierre Loti," was born in Rochefort, of an old French-Protestant family, January 14, 1850. He was connected with the. French Navy from 1867 to 1900, and is now a retired officer with full captain's rank. Although of a most energetic character and a veteran of various campaigns—Japan, Tonkin, Senegal, China (1900)—M. Viaud was so timid as a young midshipman that his comrades named him "Loti," a small Indian flower which seems ever discreetly to hide itself. This is, perhaps, a pleasantry, as elsewhere there is a much more romantic explanation of the word. Suffice it to say that Pierre Loti has been always the nom de plume of M. Viaud.

Lod has no immediate literary ancestor and no pupil worthy of the name. He indulges in a dainty pessimism and is most of all an impressionist, not of the vogue of Zola—although he can be, on occasion, as brutally plain as he—but more in the manner of Victor Hugo, his predecessor, or Alphonse Daudet, his lifelong friend. In Loti's works, however, pessimism is softened to a musical melancholy; the style is direct; the vocabulary exquisite; the moral situations familiar; the characters not complex. In short, his place is unique, apart from the normal lines of novelistic development.

The vein of Loti is not absolutely new, but is certainly novel. In him it first revealed itself in a receptive sympathy for the rare flood of experiences that his naval life brought on him, experiences which had not fallen to the lot of Bernardin de St. Pierre or Chateaubriand, both of whom he resembles. But neither of those writers possessed Loti's delicate sensitiveness to exotic nature as it is reflected in the foreign mind and heart. Strange but real worlds he has conjured up for us in most of his works and with means that are, as with all great artists, extremely simple. He may be compared to Kipling and to Stevenson: to Kipling, because he has done for the French seaman something that the Englishman has done for "Tommy Atkins," although their methods are often more opposed than similar; like Stevenson, he has gone searching for romance in the ends of the earth; like Stevenson, too, he has put into all of his works a style that is never less than dominant and often irresistible. Charm, indeed, is the one fine quality that all his critics, whether friendly or not, acknowledge, and it is one well able to cover, if need be, a multitude of literary sins.

Pierre Loti was elected a member of the French Academy in 1891, succeeding to the chair of Octave Feuillet. Some of his writings are: 'Aziyade,' written in 1879; the scene is laid in Constantinople. This was followed by 'Rarahu,' a Polynesian idyl (1880; again published under the title Le Mariage de Loti, 1882). 'Roman d'un Spahi (1881) deals with Algiers. Taton-gaye is a true 'bete-humaine', sunk in moral slumber or quivering with ferocious joys. It is in this book that Loti has eclipsed Zola. One of his masterpieces is 'Mon Freye Yves' (ocean and Brittany), together with 'Pecheur d'Islande' (1886); both translated into German by Elizabeth, Queen of Roumania (Carmen Sylva). In 1884 was published 'Les trois Dames de la Kasbah,' relating also to Algiers, and then came 'Madame Chrysantheme' (1887), crowned by the Academy. 'Japoneries d'automne' (1889), Japanese scenes; then 'Au Maroc' (Morocco; 1890). Partly autobiographical are 'Le Roman d'un Enfant' (1890) and 'Le Livre de la Pitie et de la Mort' (1891). Then followed 'Fantomes d'Orient (1892), L'Exilee (1893), Le Desert (Syria; 1895), Jerusalem, La Galilee (Palestine; 1895), Pages choisies (1896), Ramuntcho (1897), Reflets sur la Sombre Route' (1898), and finally 'Derniers Jours de Pekin' (1903). Many exquisite pages are to be found in Loti's work. His composition is now and then somewhat disconnected; the impressions are vague, almost illusory, and the mirage is a little obscure, but the intense and abiding charm of Nature remains. Loti has not again reached the level of Madame Chrysantheme, and English critics at least will have to suspend their judgment for a while. In any event, he has given to the world many great books, and is shrined with the Forty "Immortals."

ALBERT SOREL

of the French Academy.

À MADAME
LA DUCHESSE DE RICHELIEU

Permit me to beg your acceptance of this work, as a respectful tribute of my friendship.

I feel some hesitation in offering it, for its theme can not be deemed altogether correct; but I have endeavored to make its expression, at least, in harmony with good taste, and I trust that my endeavors have been successful.

This record is the journal of a summer of my life, in which I have changed nothing, not even the dates, thinking that in our efforts to arrange matters we succeed often only in disarranging them. Although the most important role may appear to devolve on Madame Chrysantheme, it is very certain that the three principal points of interest are myself, Japan, and the effect produced on me by that country.

Do you recollect a certain photograph—rather absurd, I must admit— representing that great fellow Yves, a Japanese girl, and myself, grouped as we were posed by a Nagasaki artist? You smiled when I assured you that the carefully attired little damsel placed between us had been one of our neighbors. Kindly receive my book with the same indulgent smile, without seeking therein a meaning either good or bad, in the same spirit in which you would receive some quaint bit of pottery, some grotesquely carved ivory idol, or some fantastic trifle brought to you from this singular fatherland of all fantasy.

Believe me, with the deepest respect,
Madame la Duchesse,
Your affectionate
PIERRE LOTI.

FOREWORD

We were at sea, about two o'clock in the morning, on a fine night, under a starry sky.

Yves stood beside me on the bridge, and we talked of the country, unknown to both, to which destiny was now carrying us. As we were to cast anchor the next day, we enjoyed our anticipations, and made a thousand plans.

"For myself," I said, "I shall marry at once."

"Ah!" said Yves, with the indifferent air of one whom nothing can surprise.

"Yes—I shall choose a little, creamy-skinned woman with black hair and cat's eyes. She must be pretty and not much bigger than a doll. You shall have a room in our house. It will be a little paper house, in a green garden, deeply shaded. We shall live among flowers, everything around us shall blossom, and each morning our dwelling shall be filled with nosegays—nosegays such as you have never dreamed of."

Yves now began to take an interest in these plans for my future household; indeed, he would have listened with as much confidence if I had expressed the intention of taking temporary vows in some monastery of this new country, or of marrying some island queen and shutting myself up with her in a house built of jade, in the middle of an enchanted lake.

I had quite made up my mind to carry out the scheme I had unfolded to him. Yes, led on by ennui and solitude, I had gradually arrived at dreaming of and looking forward to such a marriage. And then, above all, to live for awhile on land, in some shady nook, amid trees and flowers! How tempting it sounded after the long months we had been wasting at the Pescadores (hot and arid islands, devoid of freshness, woods, or streamlets, full of faint odors of China and of death).

We had made great way in latitude since our vessel had quitted that Chinese furnace, and the constellations in the sky had undergone a series of rapid changes; the Southern Cross had disappeared at the same time as the other austral stars; and the Great Bear, rising on the horizon, was almost on as high a level as it is in the sky above France. The evening breeze soothed and revived us, bringing back to us the memory of our summer-night watches on the coast of Brittany.

What a distance we were, however, from those familiar coasts! What a tremendous distance !

I

THE MYSTERIOUS LAND

At dawn we beheld Japan.

Precisely at the foretold moment the mysterious land arose before us, afar off, like a black dot in the vast sea, which for so many days had been but a blank space.

At first we saw nothing by the rays of the rising sun but a series of tiny pink-tipped heights (the Fukai Islands). Soon, however, appeared all along the horizon, like a misty veil over the waters, Japan itself; and little by little, out of the dense shadow, arose the sharp, opaque outlines of the Nagasaki[1] mountains.

The wind was dead against us, and the strong breeze, which steadily increased, seemed as if the country were blowing with all its might, in a vain effort to drive us away from its shores. The sea, the rigging, the vessel itself, all vibrated and quivered as if with emotion.

---

[1] See illustrations at the end of the book *(Editor footnote)*.

II

'ANGE SCENES

.ock in the afternoon all these far-off
.re close to us, so close that they overshadowed
. with their rocky masses and deep green thickets.

We entered a shady channel between two high ranges of mountains, oddly symmetrical—like stage scenery, very pretty, though unlike nature. It seemed as if Japan were opened to our view through an enchanted fissure, allowing us to penetrate into her very heart.

Nagasaki, as yet unseen, must be at the extremity of this long and peculiar bay. All around us was exquisitely green. The strong sea- breeze had suddenly fallen, and was succeeded by a calm; the atmosphere, now very warm, was laden with the perfume of flowers. In the valley resounded the ceaseless whirr of the cicalas, answering one another from shore to shore; the mountains reechoed with innumerable sounds; the whole country seemed to vibrate like crystal. We passed among myriads of Japanese junks, gliding softly, wafted by imperceptible breezes on the smooth water; their motion could hardly be heard, and their white sails, stretched out on yards, fell languidly in a thousand horizontal folds like window-blinds, their strangely contorted poops, rising up castle- like in the air, reminding one of the towering ships of the Middle Ages. In the midst of the verdure of this wall of mountains, they stood out with a snowy whiteness.

What a country of verdure and shade is Japan; what an unlooked-for Eden!

Beyond us, at sea, it must have been full daylight; but here, in the depths of the valley, we already felt the impression of evening; beneath the summits in full sunlight, the base of the mountains and all the thickly wooded parts near the water's edge were steeped in twilight.

The passing junks, gleaming white against the background of dark foliage, were silently and dexterously manoeuvred by small, yellow, naked men, with long hair piled up on their heads in feminine fashion. Gradually, as we advanced farther up the green channel, the perfumes became more penetrating, and the monotonous chirp of the cicalas swelled out like an orchestral crescendo. Above us, against the luminous sky, sharply delineated between the mountains, a kind of hawk hovered, screaming out, with a deep, human voice, "Ha! Ha! Ha!" its melancholy call prolonged by the echoes.

All this fresh and luxuriant nature was of a peculiar Japanese type, which seemed to impress itself even on the mountain-tops, and produced the effect of a too artificial prettiness. The trees were grouped in clusters, with the pretentious grace shown on lacquered trays. Large rocks sprang up in exaggerated shapes, side by side with rounded, lawn- like hillocks; all the incongruous elements of landscape were grouped together as if artificially created.

When we looked intently, here and there we saw, often built in counterscarp on the very brink of an abyss, some old, tiny, mysterious pagoda, half hidden in the foliage of the overhanging trees, bringing to the minds of new arrivals, like ourselves, a sense of unfamiliarity and strangeness, and the feeling that in this country the spirits, the sylvan gods, the antique symbols, faithful guardians of the woods and forests, were unknown and incomprehensible.

When Nagasaki appeared, the view was rather disappointing. Situated at the foot of green overhanging mountains, it looked like any other ordinary town. In front of it lay a tangled mass of vessels, flying all the flags of the world; steamboats, just as in any other port, with dark funnels and black smoke, and behind them quays covered with warehouses and factories; nothing was wanting in the way of ordinary, trivial, every-day objects.

Some time, when man shall have made all things alike, the earth will be a dull, tedious dwelling-place, and we shall have even to give up travelling and seeking for a change which can no longer be found.

About six o'clock we dropped anchor noisily amid the mass of vessels already in the harbor, and were immediately invaded.

We were visited by a mercantile, bustling, comical Japan, which rushed upon us in full boat-loads, in waves, like a rising sea. Little men and little women came in a continuous, uninterrupted stream, but without cries, without squabbles, noiselessly, each one making so smiling a bow that it was impossible to be angry with them, so that by reflex action we smiled and bowed also. They carried on their backs little baskets, tiny boxes, receptacles of every shape, fitting into one another in the most ingenious manner, each containing several others, and multiplying till they filled up everything, in endless number. From these they drew forth all manner of curious and unexpected things: folding screens, slippers, soap, lanterns, sleeve-links, live cicalas chirping in little cages, jewelry, tame white mice turning little cardboard mills, quaint photographs, hot soups and stews in bowls, ready to be served out in rations to the crew;—china, a legion of vases, teapots, cups, little pots and plates. In one moment, all this was unpacked, spread out with astounding rapidity and a certain talent for arrangement; each seller squatting monkey-like, hands touching feet, behind his fancy ware—always smiling, bending low with the most engaging bows. Under the mass of these many-colored things, the deck presented the appearance of an immense bazaar; the sailors, very much amused and full of fun, walked among the heaped-up piles, taking the little women by the chin, buying anything and everything; throwing broadcast their white dollars. But how ugly, mean, and grotesque all those folk were! I began to feel singularly uneasy and disenchanted regarding my possible marriage.

Yves and I were on duty till the next morning, and after the first bustle, which always takes place on board when settling down in harbor— boats to lower, booms to swing out, running rigging to make taut—we had nothing more to do but look on. We said to each other: "Where are we in reality?—In the United States?—In some English colony in Australia, or in New Zealand?"

Consular residences, custom-house offices, manufactories; a dry dock in which a Russian frigate was lying; on the heights the large European concession, sprinkled with villas, and on the quays, American bars for the sailors. Farther off, it is true, far away behind these commonplace objects, in the very depths of the vast green valley, peered thousands upon thousands of tiny black houses, a tangled mass of curious appearance, from which here and there emerged some higher, dark red, painted roofs, probably the true old Japanese Nagasaki, which still exists. And in those quarters—who knows?—

there may be, lurking behind a paper screen, some affected, cat's-eyed little woman, whom perhaps in two or three days (having no time to lose) I shall marry! But no, the picture painted by my fancy has faded. I can no longer see this little creature in my mind's eye; the sellers of the white mice have blurred her image; I fear now, lest she should be like them.

At nightfall the decks were suddenly cleared as by enchantment; in a second they had shut up their boxes, folded their sliding screens and their trick fans, and, humbly bowing to each of us, the little men and little women disappeared.

Slowly, as the shades of night closed around us, mingling all things in the bluish darkness, Japan became once more, little by little, a fairy- like and enchanted country. The great mountains, now black, were mirrored and doubled in the still water at their feet, reflecting therein their sharply reversed outlines, and presenting the mirage of fearful precipices, over which we seemed to hang. The stars also were reversed in their order, making, in the depths of the imaginary abyss, a sprinkling of tiny phosphorescent lights.

Then all Nagasaki became profusely illuminated, sparkling with multitudes of lanterns: the smallest suburb, the smallest village was lighted up; the tiniest but perched up among the trees, which in the daytime was invisible, threw out its little glowworm glimmer. Soon there were innumerable lights all over the country on all the shores of the bay, from top to bottom of the mountains; myriads of glowing fires shone out in the darkness, conveying the impression of a vast capital rising around us in one bewildering amphitheatre. Beneath, in the silent waters, another town, also illuminated, seemed to descend into the depths of the abyss. The night was balmy, pure, delicious; the atmosphere laden with the perfume of flowers came wafted to us from the mountains. From the tea-houses and other nocturnal resorts, the sound of guitars reached our ears, seeming in the distance the sweetest of music. And the whirr of the cicalas—which, in Japan, is one of the continuous noises of life, and which in a few days we shall no longer even be aware of, so completely is it the background and foundation of all other terrestrial sounds—was sonorous, incessant, softly monotonous, like the murmur of a crystal waterfall.

III

THE GARDEN OF FLOWERS

The next day the rain fell in torrents, merciless and unceasing, blinding and drenching everything—a rain so dense that it was impossible to see through it from one end of the vessel to the other. It seemed as if the clouds of the whole world had amassed themselves in Nagasaki Bay, and chosen this great green funnel to stream down. And so thickly did the rain fall that it became almost as dark as night. Through a veil of restless water, we still perceived the base of the mountains, but the summits were lost to sight among the great dark masses overshadowing us. Above us shreds of clouds, seemingly torn from the dark vault, draggled across the trees, like gray rags-continually melting away in torrents of water. The wind howled through the ravines with a deep tone. The whole surface of the bay, bespattered by the rain, flogged by the gusts of wind that blew from all quarters, splashed, moaned, and seethed in violent agitation.

What depressing weather for a first landing, and how was I to find a wife through such a deluge, in an unknown country?

No matter! I dressed myself and said to Yves, who smiled at my obstinate determination in spite of unfavorable circumstances:

"Hail me a 'sampan,' brother, please."

Yves then, by a motion of his arm through the wind and rain, summoned a kind of little, white, wooden sarcophagus which was skipping near us on the waves, sculled by two yellow boys stark naked in the rain. The craft approached us, I jumped into it, then through a little trap-door shaped like a rat-trap that one of the scullers threw open for me, I slipped in and stretched myself at full length on a mat in what is called the "cabin" of a sampan.

There was just room enough for my body to lie in this floating coffin, which was scrupulously clean, white with the whiteness of new deal boards. I was well sheltered from the rain, that fell pattering on my lid, and thus I started for the town, lying in this box, flat on my stomach, rocked by one wave, roughly shaken by another, at moments almost overturned; and through the half-opened door of my rattrap I saw, upside- down, the two little creatures to whom I had entrusted my fate, children of eight or ten years of age at the most, who, with little monkeyish faces, had, however, fully developed muscles, like miniature men, and were already as skilful as regular old salts.

Suddenly they began to shout; no doubt we were approaching the landing- place. And indeed, through my trap-door, which I had now thrown wide open, I saw quite near to me the gray flagstones on the quays. I got out of my sarcophagus and prepared to set foot on Japanese soil for the first time in my life.

All was streaming around us, and the tiresome rain dashed into my eyes.

Hardly had I landed, when there bounded toward me a dozen strange beings, of what description it was almost impossible to distinguish through the blinding rain—a species of human hedgehog, each dragging some large black object; they came screaming around me and stopped my progress. One of them opened and held over my head an enormous, closely-ribbed umbrella, decorated on its transparent surface with paintings of storks; and they all smiled at me in an engaging manner, with an air of expectation.

I had been forewarned; these were only the *djins* who were touting for the honor of my preference; nevertheless I was startled at this sudden attack, this Japanese welcome on a first visit to land (the *djins* or *djin-richisans[1]*, are the runners who drag little carts, and are paid for conveying people to and fro, being hired by the hour or the distance, as cabs are hired in Europe).

Their legs were naked; to-day they were very wet, and their heads were hidden under large, shady, conical hats. By way of waterproofs they wore nothing less than mats of straw, with all the ends of the straws turned outward, bristling like porcupines; they seemed clothed in a thatched roof. They continued to smile, awaiting my choice.

---

[1] The right word is *jinrikisha – jin, means only man (Editor footnote).*

Not having the honor of being acquainted with any of them in particular, I chose at haphazard the djin with the umbrella and got into his little cart, of which he carefully lowered the hood. He drew an oilcloth apron over my knees, pulling it up to my face, and then advancing, asked me, in Japanese, something which must have meant: "Where to, sir?" To which I replied, in the same language, "To the Garden of Flowers, my friend."

I said this in the three words I had, parrot-like, learned by heart, astonished that such sounds could mean anything, astonished, too, at their being understood. We started, he running at full speed, I dragged along and jerked about in his light chariot, wrapped in oilcloth, shut up as if in a box—both of us unceasingly drenched all the while, and dashing all around us the water and mud of the sodden ground.

"To the Garden of Flowers,[1]" I had said, like a habitual frequenter of the place, and quite surprised at hearing myself speak. But I was less ignorant about Japan than might have been supposed. Many of my friends, on their return home from that country, had told me about it, and I knew a great deal; the Garden of Flowers is a tea-house, an elegant rendezvous. There I should inquire for a certain Kangourou-San, who is at the same time interpreter, laundryman, and confidential agent for the intercourse of races. Perhaps this very evening, if all went well, I should be introduced to the bride destined for me by mysterious fate. This thought kept my mind on the alert during the panting journey we made, the djin and I, one dragging the other, under the merciless downpour.

---

[1] *Karyūkai* in Tokyo, we find also the words : "the floating world » *(Editor footnote).*

Oh, what a curious Japan I saw that day, throug
gaping of my oilcloth coverings, from under the dripp
hood of my little cart! A sullen, muddy, half-drowne
Japan. All these houses, men, and beasts, hitherto known
to me only in drawings; all these, that I had beheld
painted on blue or pink backgrounds of fans or vases,
now appeared to me in their hard reality, under a dark
sky, with umbrellas and wooden shoes, with tucked-up
skirts and pitiful aspect.

At times the rain fell so heavily that I closed up tightly
every chink and crevice, and the noise and shaking
benumbed me, so that I completely forgot in what
country I was. In the hood of the cart were holes, through
which little streams ran down my back. Then,
remembering that I was going for the first time in my life
through the very heart of Nagasaki, I cast an inquiring
look outside, at the risk of receiving a drenching: we
were trotting along through a mean, narrow, little back
street (there are thousands like it, a labyrinth of them),
the rain falling in cascades from the tops of the roofs on
the gleaming flagstones below, rendering everything
indistinct and vague through the misty atmosphere. At
times we passed a woman struggling with her skirts,
unsteadily tripping along in her high wooden shoes,
looking exactly like the figures painted on screens,
cowering under a gaudily daubed paper umbrella. Again,
we passed a pagoda, where an old granite monster,
squatting in the water, seemed to make a hideous,
ferocious grimace at me.

How large this Nagasaki is! Here had we been
running hard for the last hour, and still it seemed never-
ending. It is a flat plain, and one never would suppose
from the view in the offing that so vast a plain lies in the
depth of this valley.

r, have been impossible for me to
in what direction we had run; I
y djin and to my good luck.

gine of a man my djin was! I had
med to the Chinese runners, but they were
g beside this fellow. When I part my oilcloth to
peep at anything, he is naturally always the first object in
my foreground; his two naked, brown, muscular legs,
scampering along, splashing all around, and his bristling
hedgehog back bending low in the rain. Do the passers-
by, gazing at this little dripping cart, guess that it contains
a suitor in quest of a bride?

At last my vehicle stops, and my djin, with many
smiles and precautions lest any fresh rivers should stream
down my back, lowers the hood of the cart; there is a
break in the storm, and the rain has ceased. I had not yet
seen his face; as an exception to the general rule, he is
good- looking; a young man of about thirty years of age,
of intelligent and strong appearance, and a frank
countenance. Who could have foreseen that a few days
later this very djin? But no, I will not anticipate, and run
the risk of throwing beforehand any discredit on
Chrysantheme.

We had therefore reached our destination, and found
ourselves at the foot of a high, overhanging mountain;
probably beyond the limits of the town, in some suburban
district. It apparently became necessary to continue our
journey on foot, and to climb up an almost perpendicular
narrow path.

Around us, a number of small country-houses, garden-
walls, and high bamboo palisades shut off the view. The
green hill crushed us with its towering height; the heavy,
dark clouds lowering over our heads seemed like a leaden

canopy confining us in this unknown spot; it really seemed as if the complete absence of perspective inclined one all the better to notice the details of this tiny corner, muddy and wet, of homely Japan, now lying before our eyes. The earth was very red. The grasses and wild flowers bordering the pathway were strange to me; nevertheless, the palings were covered with convolvuli like our own, and I recognized china asters, zinnias, and other familiar flowers in the gardens. The atmosphere seemed laden with a curiously complicated odor, something besides the perfume of the plants and soil, arising no doubt from the human dwelling-places—a mingled odor, I fancied, of dried fish and incense. Not a creature was to be seen; of the inhabitants, of their homes and life, there was not a vestige, and I might have imagined myself anywhere in the world.

My djin had fastened his little cart under a tree, and together we climbed the steep path on the slippery red soil.

"We are going to the Garden of Flowers, are we not?" I inquired, desirous to ascertain whether I had been understood.

"Yes, yes," replied the djin, "it is up there, and quite near."

The road turned, steep banks hemming it in and darkening it. On one side it skirted the mountain, all covered with a tangle of wet ferns; on the other appeared a large wooden house almost devoid of openings and of evil aspect; it was there that my djin halted.

What, was that sinister-looking house the Garden of Flowers? He assured me that it was, and seemed very sure of the fact. We knocked at a large door which opened immediately, slipping back in its groove. Then two funny little women appeared, oldish-looking, but with evident pretensions to youth: exact types of the figures painted on vases, with their tiny hands and feet.

On catching sight of me they threw themselves on all fours, their faces touching the floor. Good gracious! What can be the matter? I asked myself. Nothing at all, it was only the ceremonious salute, to which I am as yet unaccustomed. They arose, and proceeded to take off my boots (one never keeps on one's shoes in a Japanese house), wiping the bottoms of my trousers, and feeling my shoulders to see whether I am wet.

What always strikes one on first entering a Japanese dwelling is the extreme cleanliness, the white and chilling bareness of the rooms.

Over the most irreproachable mattings, without a crease, a line, or a stain, I was led upstairs to the first story and ushered into a large, empty room—absolutely empty! The paper walls were mounted on sliding panels, which, fitting into each other, can be made to disappear— and all one side of the apartment opened like a veranda, giving a view of the green country and the gray sky beyond. By way of a chair, they gave me a square cushion of black velvet; and behold me seated low, in the middle of this large, empty room, which by its very vastness is almost chilly. The two little women (who are the servants of the house and my very humble servants, too), awaited my orders, in attitudes expressive of the profoundest humility.

It seemed extraordinary that the quaint words, the curious phrases I had learned during our exile at the Pescadores Islands—by sheer dint of dictionary and grammar, without attaching the least sense to them—

should mean anything. But so it seemed, however, for I was at once understood.

I wished in the first place to speak to one M. Kangourou, who is interpreter, laundryman, and matrimonial agent. Nothing could be easier: they knew him and were willing to go at once in search of him; and the elder of the waiting-maids made ready for the purpose her wooden clogs and her paper umbrella.

Next I demanded a well-served repast, composed of the greatest delicacies of Japan. Better and better! they rushed to the kitchen to order it.

Finally, I beg they will give tea and rice to my djin, who is waiting for me below; I wish,—in short, I wish many things, my dear little dolls, which I will mention by degrees and with due deliberation, when I shall have had time to assemble the necessary words. But the more I look at you the more uneasy I feel as to what my fiancee of to-morrow may be like. Almost pretty, I grant you, you are—in virtue of quaintness, delicate hands, miniature feet, but ugly, after all, and absurdly small. You look like little monkeys, like little china ornaments, like I don't know what. I begin to understand that I have arrived at this house at an ill-chosen moment. Something is going on which does not concern me, and I feel that I am in the way.

From the beginning I might have guessed as much, notwithstanding the excessive politeness of my welcome; for I remember now, that while they were taking off my boots downstairs, I heard a murmuring chatter overhead, then a noise of panels moved quickly along their grooves, evidently to hide from me something not intended for me to see; they were improvising for me the apartment in which I now am just as in menageries they make a separate compartment for some beasts when the public is admitted.

Now I am left alone while my orders are being executed, and I listen attentively, squatted like a Buddha on my black velvet cushion, in the midst of the whiteness of the walls and mats.

Behind the paper partitions, feeble voices, seemingly numerous, are talking in low tones. Then rises the sound of a guitar[1], and the song of a woman, plaintive and gentle in the echoing sonority of the bare house, in the melancholy of the rainy weather.

What one can see through the wide-open veranda is very pretty; I will admit that it resembles the landscape of a fairytale. There are admirably wooded mountains, climbing high into the dark and gloomy sky, and hiding in it the peaks of their summits, and, perched up among the clouds, is a temple. The atmosphere has that absolute transparency, that distance and clearness which follows a great fall of rain; but a thick pall, still heavy with moisture, remains suspended over all, and on the foliage of the hanging woods still float great flakes of gray fluff, which remain there, motionless. In the foreground, in front of and below this almost fantastic landscape, is a miniature garden where two beautiful white cats are taking the air, amusing themselves by pursuing each other through the paths of a Lilliputian labyrinth, shaking the wet sand from their paws. The garden is as conventional as possible: not a flower, but little rocks, little lakes, dwarf trees cut in grotesque fashion; all this is not natural, but it is most ingeniously arranged, so green, so full of fresh mosses!

---

[1] Probably a shamisen *(Editor footnote)*.

In the rain-soaked country below me, to the very farthest end of the vast scene, reigns a great silence, an absolute calm. But the woman's voice, behind the paper wall, continues to sing in a key of gentle sadness, and the accompanying guitar has sombre and even gloomy notes.

Stay, though! Now the music is somewhat quicker—one might even suppose they were dancing!

So much the worse! I shall try to look between the fragile divisions, through a crack which has revealed itself to my notice.

What a singular spectacle it is; evidently the gilded youth of Nagasaki holding a great clandestine orgy! In an apartment as bare as my own, there are a dozen of them, seated in a circle on the ground, attired in long blue cotton dresses with pagoda sleeves, long, sleek, and greasy hair surmounted by European pot-hats; and beneath these, yellow, worn- out, bloodless, foolish faces. On the floor are a number of little spirit-lamps, little pipes, little lacquer trays, little teapots, little cups-all the accessories and all the remains of a Japanese feast, resembling nothing so much as a doll's tea-party. In the midst of this circle of dandies are three overdressed women, one might say three weird visions, robed in garments of pale and indefinable colors, embroidered with golden monsters; their great coiffures are arranged with fantastic art, stuck full of pins and flowers. Two are seated with their backs turned to me: one is holding the guitar, the other singing with that soft, pretty voice; thus seen furtively, from behind, their pose, their hair, the nape of their necks, all is exquisite, and I tremble lest a movement should reveal to me faces which might destroy the enchantment. The third girl is on her feet, dancing before this areopagus of idiots, with their lanky locks and pot-hats. What a shock when she turns round! She wears over her face the horribly grinning, death-like mask of a spectre or a vampire. The mask unfastened, falls. And behold! a darling little fairy of about twelve or fifteen years of age, slim, and already a coquette, already a woman—dressed in a long robe of shaded dark-blue china crape, covered with embroidery representing bats-gray bats, black bats, golden bats.

Suddenly there are steps on the stairs, the light foot steps of barefooted women pattering over the white mats. No doubt the first course of my luncheon is just about to be served. I fall back quickly, fixed and motionless, upon my black velvet cushion. There are three of them now, three waiting-maids who arrive in single file, with smiles and curtseys. One offers me the spirit-lamp and the teapot; another, preserved fruits in delightful little plates; the third, absolutely indefinable objects upon gems of little trays. And they grovel before me on the floor, placing all this plaything of a meal at my feet.

At this moment, my impressions of Japan are charming enough; I feel myself fairly launched upon this tiny, artificial, fictitious world, which I felt I knew already from the paintings on lacquer and porcelains. It is so exact a representation! The three little squatting women, graceful and dainty, with their narrow slits of eyes, their magnificent coiffures in huge bows, smooth and shining as shoe-polish, and the little tea-service on the floor, the landscape seen through the veranda, the pagoda perched among the clouds; and over all the same affectation everywhere, in every detail. Even the woman's melancholy voice, still to be heard behind the paper partition, was evidently the proper way for them to sing—these musicians I had so often seen painted in amazing colors on rice-paper, half closing their dreamy eyes among impossibly large flowers. Long before I arrived there, I had perfectly pictured Japan to myself. Nevertheless, in the reality it almost seems to be smaller, more finicking than I had imagined it, and also much more mournful, no doubt by reason of that great pall of black clouds hanging over us, and this incessant rain.

While awaiting M. Kangourou (who is dressing himself, it appears, and will be here shortly), it may be as well to begin luncheon.

In the daintiest bowl imaginable, adorned with flights of storks, is the most wildly impossible soup made of seaweed. After which there are little fish dried in sugar, crabs in sugar, beans in sugar, and fruits in vinegar and pepper. All this is atrocious, but above all unexpected and unimaginable. The little women make me eat, laughing much, with that perpetual, irritating laugh which is peculiar to Japan—they make me eat, according to their fashion, with dainty chop-sticks, fingered with affected grace. I am becoming accustomed to their faces. The whole effect is refined—a refinement so entirely different from our own that at first sight I understand nothing of it, although in the long run it may end by pleasing me.

Suddenly enters, like a night butterfly awakened in broad daylight, like a rare and surprising moth, the dancing-girl from the other compartment, the child who wore the horrible mask. No doubt she wishes to have a look at me. She rolls her eyes like a timid kitten, and then all at once tamed, nestles against me, with a coaxing air of childishness, which is a delightfully transparent assumption. She is slim, elegant, delicate, and smells sweet; she is drolly painted, white as plaster, with a little circle of rouge marked very precisely in the middle of each cheek, the mouth reddened, and a touch of gilding outlining the under lip. As they could not whiten the back of her neck on account of all the delicate little curls of hair growing there, they had, in their love of exactitude, stopped the white plaster in a straight line, which might have been cut with a knife, and in consequence at the nape appears a square of natural skin of a deep yellow.

An imperious note sounds on the guitar, evidently a summons! Crac! Away she goes, the little fairy, to entertain the drivelling fools on the other side of the screens.

Suppose I marry this one, without seeking any further. I should respect her as a child committed to my care; I should take her for what she is: a fantastic and charming plaything. What an amusing little household I should set up! Really, short of marrying a china ornament, I should find it difficult to choose better.

At this moment enters M. Kangourou, clad in a suit of gray tweed, which might have come from La Belle Jardiniere or the Pont Neuf, with a pot-hat and white thread gloves. His countenance is at once foolish and cunning; he has hardly any nose or eyes. He makes a real Japanese salutation: an abrupt dip, the hands placed flat on the knees, the body making a right angle to the legs, as if the fellow were breaking in two; a little snake- like hissing (produced by sucking the saliva between the teeth, which is the highest expression of obsequious politeness in this country).

"You speak French, Monsieur Kangourou?"

"Yes, Monsieur" (renewed bows).

He makes one for each word I utter, as if he were a mechanical toy pulled by a string; when he is seated before me on the ground, he limits himself to a duck of the head—always accompanied by the same hissing noise of the saliva.

"A cup of tea, Monsieur Kangourou?"

Fresh salute and an extra affected gesticulation with the hands, as if to say, "I should hardly dare. It is too great a condescension on your part. However, anything to oblige you."

He guesses at the first words what I require from him.

"Of course," he replies, "we shall see about it at once. In a week's time, as it happens, a family from Simonoseki, in which there are two charming daughters, will be here!"

"What! in a week! You don't know me, Monsieur Kangourou! No, no, either now, to-morrow, or not at all."

Again a hissing bow, and Kangourou-San, understanding my agitation, begins to pass in feverish review all the young persons at his disposal in Nagasaki.

"Let us see—there was Mademoiselle Oeillet. What a pity that you did not speak a few days sooner! So pretty! So clever at playing the guitar! It is an irreparable misfortune; she was engaged only yesterday by a Russian officer.

"Ah! Mademoiselle Abricot!—Would she suit you, Mademoiselle Abricot? She is the daughter of a wealthy China merchant in the Decima Bazaar, a person of the highest merit; but she would be very dear: her parents, who think a great deal of her, will not let her go under a hundred yen— [A yen is equal to four shillings.]—a month. She is very accomplished, thoroughly understands commercial writing, and has at her fingers'-ends more than two thousand characters of learned writing. In a poetical competition she gained the first prize with a sonnet composed in praise of 'the blossoms of the blackthorn hedges seen in the dew of early morning.' Only, she is not very pretty: one of her eyes is smaller than the other, and she has a hole in her cheek, resulting from an illness of her childhood."

"Oh, no! on no account that one! Let us seek among a less distinguished class of young persons, but without scars. And how about those on the other side of the screen, in those fine gold-embroidered dresses? For instance, the dancer with the spectre mask, Monsieur Kangourou? or again she who sings in so dulcet a strain and has such a charming nape to her neck?"

He does not, at first, understand my drift; then when he gathers my meaning, he shakes his head almost in a joking way, and says:

"No, Monsieur, no! Those are only geishas,—[Geishas are professional dancers and singers trained at the Yeddo Conservatory.]—Monsieur— geishas!"

"Well, but why not a geisha? What difference can it make to me whether they are geishas or not?" Later, no doubt, when I understand Japanese affairs better, I shall appreciate myself the enormity of my proposal: one would really suppose I had talked of marrying the devil.

At this point M. Kangourou suddenly calls to mind one Mademoiselle Jasmin. Heavens! how was it he had not thought of her at once? She is absolutely and exactly what I want; he will go to-morrow, or this very evening, to make the necessary overtures to the parents of this young person, who live a long way off, on the opposite hill, in the suburb of Diou-djen-dji. She is a very pretty girl of about fifteen. She can probably be engaged for about eighteen or twenty dollars a month, on condition of presenting her with a few costumes of the best fashion, and of lodging her in a pleasant and well-situated house—all of which a man of gallantry like myself could not fail to do.

Well, let us fix upon Mademoiselle Jasmin, then—and now we must part; time presses. M. Kangourou will come on board to-morrow to communicate to me the result of his first proceedings and to arrange with me for the interview. For the present he refuses to accept any remuneration; but I am to give him my washing, and to procure him the custom of my brother officers of the 'Triomphante.' It is all settled. Profound bows—they put on my boots again at the door. My djin, profiting by the interpreter kind fortune has placed in his way, begs to be recommended to me for future custom; his stand is on the quay; his number is 415, inscribed in French characters on the lantern of his vehicle (we have a number 415 on board, one Le Goelec, gunner, who serves the left of one of my guns; happy thought! I shall remember this); his price is sixpence the journey, or five-pence an hour, for his customers. Capital! he shall have my custom, that is promised. And now, let us be off. The waiting- maids, who have escorted me to the door, fall on all fours as a final salute, and remain prostrate on the threshold as long as I am still in sight down the dark pathway, where the rain trickles off the great overarching bracken upon my head.

IV

CHOOSING A BRIDE

Three days have passed. Night is closing, in an apartment which has been mine since yesterday. Yves and I, on the first floor, move restlessly over the white mats, striding to and fro in the great bare room, of which the thin, dry flooring cracks beneath our footsteps; we are both rather irritated by prolonged expectation. Yves, whose impatience shows itself more freely, from time to time looks out of the window. As for myself, a chill suddenly seizes me, at the idea that I have chosen to inhabit this lonely house, lost in the midst of the suburb of a totally strange town, perched high on the mountain and almost opening upon the woods.

What wild notion could have taken possession of me, to settle myself in surroundings so foreign and unknown, breathing of isolation and sadness? The waiting unnerves me, and I beguile the time by examining all the little details of the building. The woodwork of the ceiling is complicated and ingenious. On the partitions of white paper which form the walls, are scattered tiny, microscopic, blue-feathered tortoises.

"They are late," said Yves, who is still looking out into the street.

As to being late, that they certainly are, by a good hour already, and night is falling, and the boat which should take us back to dine on board will be gone. Probably we shall have to sup Japanese fashion tonight, heaven only knows where. The people of this country have no sense of punctuality, or of the value of time.

Therefore I continue to inspect the minute and comical details of my dwelling. Here, instead of handles such as we should have made to pull these movable partitions, they have made little oval-holes, just the shape of a finger-end, into which one is evidently to put one's thumb. These little holes have a bronze ornamentation, and, on looking closely, one sees that the bronze is curiously chased: here is a lady fanning herself; there, in the next hole, is represented a branch of cherry in full blossom. What eccentricity there is in the taste of this people! To bestow assiduous labor on such miniature work, and then to hide it at the bottom of a hole to put one's finger in, looking like a mere spot in the middle of a great white panel; to accumulate so much patient and delicate workmanship on almost imperceptible accessories, and all to produce an effect which is absolutely nil, an effect of the most complete bareness and nudity.

Yves still continues to gaze forth, like Sister Anne. From the side on which he leans, my veranda overlooks a street, or rather a road bordered with houses, which climbs higher and higher, and loses itself almost immediately in the verdure of the mountain, in the fields of tea, the underwood and the cemeteries. As for myself, this delay finally irritates me thoroughly, and I turn my glances to the opposite side. The other end of my house, also a veranda, opens first of all upon a garden; then upon a marvellous panorama of woods and mountains, with all the venerable Japanese quarters of Nagasaki lying confusedly like a black ant-heap, six hundred feet below us. This evening, in a dull twilight, notwithstanding that it is a twilight of July, these things are melancholy. Great clouds heavy with rain and showers, ready to fall, are travelling across the sky. No, I can not feel at home in this strange dwelling I have chosen; I feel sensations of extreme solitude and strangeness; the mere prospect of passing the night in it gives me a shudder of horror.

"Ah! at last, brother," said Yves, "I believe—yes, I really believe she is coming at last."

I look over his shoulder, and I see a back view of a little doll, the finishing touches to whose toilette are being put in the solitary street; a last maternal glance is given the enormous bows of the sash, the folds at the waist. Her dress is of pearl-gray silk, her obi (sash) of mauve satin; a sprig of silver flowers trembles in her black hair; a parting ray of sunlight touches the little figure; five or six persons accompany her. Yes! it is undoubtedly Mademoiselle Jasmin; they are bringing me my fiancee!

I rush to the ground floor, inhabited by old Madame Prune, my landlady, and her aged husband; they are absorbed in prayer before the altar of their ancestors.

"Here they are, Madame Prune," I cry in Japanese; "here they are! Bring at once the tea, the lamp, the embers, the little pipes for the ladies, the little bamboo pots! Bring up, as quickly as possible, all the accessories for my reception!"

I hear the front door open, and hasten upstairs again. Wooden clogs are deposited on the floor, the staircase creaks gently under little bare feet. Yves and I look at each other, with a longing to laugh.

An old lady enters—two old ladies—three old ladies, emerging from the doorway one after another with jerking and mechanical salutations, which we return as best we can, fully conscious of our inferiority in this particular style. Then come persons of intermediate age—then quite young ones, a dozen at least, friends, neighbors, the whole quarter, in fact. And the entire company, on arriving, becomes confusedly engaged in reciprocal salutations: I salute you—you salute me—I salute you again, and you return it—and I re-salute you again, and I express that I shall never, never be able to return it according to your high merit—and I bang my forehead against the ground, and you stick your nose between the planks of the flooring, and there they are, on all fours one before another; it is a polite dispute, all eager to yield precedence as to sitting down, or passing first, and compliments without end are murmured in low tones, with faces against the floor.

They seat themselves at last, smiling, in a ceremonious circle; we two remaining standing, our eyes fixed on the staircase. And at length emerges the little aigrette of silver flowers, the ebony coiffure, the gray silk robe and mauve sash of Mademoiselle Jasmin, my fiancee!

Heavens! why, I know her already! Long before setting foot in Japan, I had met her, on every fan, on every teacup with her silly air, her puffy little face, her tiny eyes, mere gimlet-holes above those expanses of impossible pink and white cheeks.

She is young, that is all I can say in her favor; she is even so young that I should almost scruple to accept her. The wish to laugh leaves me suddenly, and instead, a profound chill seizes my heart. What! share even an hour of my life with that little doll? Never!

The next question is, how to get rid of her.

She advances smiling, with an air of repressed triumph, and behind her looms M. Kangourou, in his suit of gray tweed. Fresh salutes, and behold her on all fours, she too, before my landlady and before my neighbors. Yves, the big Yves, who is not about to be married, stands behind me, with a comical grimace, hardly repressing his laughter—while to give myself time to collect my ideas, I offer tea in little cups, little spittoons, and embers to the company.

Nevertheless, my discomfited air does not escape my visitors.
M. Kangourou anxiously inquires:

"How do you like her?" And I reply in a low voice, but with great resolution:

"Not at all! I won't have that one. Never!"

I believe that this remark was almost understood in the circle around me. Consternation was depicted on every face, jaws dropped, and pipes went out. And now I address my reproaches to Kangourou: "Why have you brought her to me in such pomp, before friends and neighbors of both sexes, instead of showing her to me discreetly, as if by chance, as I had wished? What an affront you will compel me now to put upon all these polite persons!"

The old ladies (the mamma, no doubt, and aunts), prick up their ears, and M. Kangourou translates to them, softening as much as possible, my heartrending decision. I feel really almost sorry for them; the fact is, that for women who, not to put too fine a point upon it, have come to sell a child, they have an air I was not prepared for: I can hardly say an air of respectability (a word in use with us which is absolutely without meaning in Japan), but an air of unconscious and good-natured simplicity. They are only doing a thing that is perfectly admissible in their world, and really it all resembles, more than I could have thought possible, a bona fide marriage.

"But what fault do you find with the little girl?" asks M. Kangourou, in consternation.

I endeavor to present the matter in the most flattering light:

"She is very young," I say; "and then she is too white, too much like our own women. I wished for one with an ivory skin, just as a change."

"But that is only the paint they have put on her, Monsieur!   Beneath   it, I assure you, she is of an ivory hue."

Yves leans toward me and whispers:

"Look over there, brother, in that corner by the last panel; have you noticed the one who is sitting down?"

Not I. In my annoyance I had not observed her; she had her back to the light, was dressed in dark colors, and sat in the careless attitude of one who keeps in the background. The fact is, this one pleased me much better. Eyes with long lashes, rather narrow, but which would have been called good in any country in the world; with almost an expression, almost a thought. A coppery tint on her rounded cheeks; a straight nose; slightly thick lips, but well modelled and with pretty corners. A little older than Mademoiselle Jasmin, about eighteen years of age perhaps, already more of a woman. She wore an expression of ennui, also of a little contempt, as if she regretted her attendance at a spectacle which dragged so much, and was so little amusing.

"Monsieur Kangourou, who is that young lady over there, in dark blue?"

"Over there, Monsieur? She is called Mademoiselle Chrysantheme. She came with the others you see here; she is only here as a spectator. She pleases you?" said he, with eager suddenness, espying a way out of his difficulty. Then, forgetting all his politeness, all his ceremoniousness, all his Japanesery, he takes her by the hand, forces her to rise, to stand in the dying daylight, to let herself be seen. And she, who has followed our eyes and begins to guess what is on foot, lowers her head in confusion, with a more decided but more charming pout, and tries to step back, half-sulky, half-smiling.

"It makes no difference," continues M. Kangourou, "it can be arranged just as well with this one; she is not married either, Monsieur!"

She is not married! Then why didn't the idiot propose her to me at once instead of the other, for whom I have a feeling of the greatest pity, poor little soul, with her pearl-gray dress, her sprig of flowers, her now sad and mortified expression, and her eyes which twinkle like those of a child about to cry.

"It can be arranged, Monsieur!" repeats Kangourou again, who at this moment appears to me a go-between of the lowest type, a rascal of the meanest kind.

Only, he adds, we, Yves and I, are in the way during the negotiations. And, while Mademoiselle Chrysantheme remains with her eyelids lowered, as befits the occasion, while the various families, on whose countenances may be read every degree of astonishment, every phase of expectation, remain seated in a circle on my white mats, he sends us two into the veranda, and we gaze down into the depths below us, upon a misty and vague Nagasaki, a Nagasaki melting into a blue haze of darkness.

Then ensue long discourses in Japanese, arguments without end. M. Kangourou, who is laundryman and low scamp in French only, has returned for these discussions to the long formulas of his country. From time to time I express impatience, I ask this worthy creature, whom I am less and less able to consider in a serious light:

"Come now, tell us frankly, Kangourou, are we any nearer coming to some arrangement? Is all this ever going to end?"

"In a moment, Monsieur, in a moment;" and he resumes his air of political economist seriously debating social problems.

Well, one must submit to the slowness of this people. And, while the darkness falls like a veil over the Japanese town, I have leisure to reflect, with as much melancholy as I please, upon the bargain that is being concluded behind me.

Night has closed in; it has been necessary to light the lamps.

It is ten o'clock when all is finally settled, and M. Kangourou comes to tell me:

"All is arranged, Monsieur: her parents will give her up for twenty dollars a month—the same price as Mademoiselle Jasmin."

On hearing this, I am possessed suddenly with extreme vexation that I should have made up my mind so quickly to link myself in ever so fleeting and transient a manner with this little creature, and dwell with her in this isolated house.

We return to the room; she is the centre of the circle and seated; and they have placed the aigrette of flowers in her hair. There is actually some expression in her glance, and I am almost persuaded that she—this one—thinks.

Yves is astonished at her modest attitude, at her little timid airs of a young girl on the verge of matrimony; he had imagined nothing like it in such a connection as this, nor I either, I must confess.

"She is really very pretty, brother," said he; "very pretty, take my word for it!"

These good folks, their customs, this scene, strike him dumb with astonishment; he can not get over it, and remains in a maze. "Oh! this is too much," he says, and the idea of writing a long letter to his wife at Toulven, describing it all, diverts him greatly.

Chrysantheme and I join hands. Yves, too, advances and touches the dainty little paw. After all, if I wed her, it is chiefly his fault; I never should have remarked her without his observation that she was pretty. Who can tell how this strange arrangement will turn out? Is it a woman or a doll? Well, time will show.

The families, having lighted their many-colored lanterns swinging at the ends of slight sticks, prepare to retire with many compliments, bows, and curtseys. When it is a question of descending the stairs, no one is willing to go first, and at a given moment, the whole party are again on all fours, motionless and murmuring polite phrases in undertones.

"Haul back there!" said Yves, laughing, and employing a nautical term used when there is a stoppage of any kind.

At length they all melt away, descending the stairs with a last buzzing accompaniment of civilities and polite phrases finished from one step to another in voices which gradually die away. He and I remain alone in the unfriendly, empty apartment, where the mats are still littered with the little cups of tea, the absurd little pipes, and the miniature trays.

"Let us watch them go away!" said Yves, leaning out. At the door of the garden is a renewal of the same salutations and curtseys, and then the two groups of women separate, their bedaubed paper lanterns fade away trembling in the distance, balanced at the extremity of flexible canes which they hold in their fingertips as one would hold a fishing-rod in the dark to catch night-birds. The procession of the unfortunate Mademoiselle Jasmin mounts upward toward the mountain, while that of Mademoiselle Chrysantheme winds downward by a narrow old street, half- stairway, half-goat-path, which leads to the town.

Then we also depart. The night is fresh, silent, exquisite, the eternal song of the cicalas fills the air. We can still see the red lanterns of my new family, dwindling away in the distance, as they descend and gradually become lost in that yawning abyss, at the bottom of which lies Nagasaki.

Our way, too, lies downward, but on an opposite slope by steep paths leading to the sea.

And when I find myself once more on board, when the scene enacted on the hill above recurs to my mind, it seems to me that my betrothal is a joke, and my new family a set of puppets.

V

A FANTASTIC MARRIAGE

July 10, 1885.

Three days have passed since my marriage was an accomplished fact.

In the lower part of the town, in one of the new cosmopolitan districts, in an ugly, pretentious building, which is a sort of registry office, the deed was signed and countersigned, with marvellous hieroglyphics, in a large book, in the presence of those absurd little creatures, formerly silken-robed Samurai, but now called policemen, dressed up in tight jackets and Russian caps.

The ceremony took place in the full heat of midday; Chrysantheme and her mother arrived together, and I alone. We seemed to have met for the purpose of ratifying some discreditable contract, and the two women trembled in the presence of these ugly little men, who, in their eyes, were the personification of the law.

In the middle of their official scrawl, they made me write in French my name, Christian name, and profession. Then they gave me an extraordinary document on a sheet of rice-paper, which set forth the permission granted me by the civilian authorities of the island of Kiu-Siu, to inhabit a house situated in the suburb of Diou-djen-dji, with a person called Chrysantheme, the said permission being under the protection of the police during the whole of my stay in Japan.

In the evening, however, in our own quarter, our little marriage became a very pretty affair—a procession carrying lanterns, a festive tea and some music. All this seemed quite necessary.

Now we are almost an old married couple, and we are gently settling down into everyday habits.

Chrysantheme tends the flowers in our bronze vases, dresses herself with studied care, proud of her socks with the divided big toe, and strums all day on a kind of long-necked guitar, producing sweet and plaintive sounds.

VI

MY NEW MENAGE

In our home, everything looks like a Japanese picture: we have folding- screens, little odd-shaped stools bearing vases full of flowers, and at the farther end of the apartment, in a nook forming a kind of altar, a large gilded Buddha sits enthroned in a lotus.

The house is just as I had fancied it should be in the many dreams of Japan I had had before my arrival, during the long night watches: perched on high, in a peaceful suburb, in the midst of green gardens; made up of paper panels, and taken to pieces according to one's fancy, like a child's toy. Whole families of cicalas chirp day and night under our old resounding roof. From our veranda we have a bewildering bird's-eye view of Nagasaki, of its streets, its junks, and its great pagodas, which, at certain hours, is illuminated at our feet like some scene in fairyland.

VII

THE LADIES OF THE FANS

Regarded as a mere outline, little Chrysantheme has been seen everywhere and by everybody. Whoever has looked at one of those paintings on china or silk that are sold in our bazaars, knows perfectly the pretty, stiff head-dress, the leaning figure, ever ready to try some new gracious salutation, the sash fastened behind in an enormous bow, the large, flowing sleeves, the drapery slightly clinging about the ankles with a little crooked train like a lizard's tail.

But her face—no, not every one has seen that; there is something special about it.

Moreover, the type of women the Japanese paint mostly on their vases is an exceptional one in their country. It is almost exclusively among the nobility that these personages are found, with their long, pale faces, painted in tender rose-tints, and silly, long necks which give them the appearance of storks. This distinguished type (which I am obliged to admit was also Mademoiselle Jasmin's) is rare, particularly at Nagasaki.

Among the middle classes and the common people, the ugliness is more pleasant and sometimes becomes a kind of prettiness. The eyes are still too small and hardly able to open, but the faces are rounder, browner, more vivacious; and in the women remains a certain vagueness of feature, something childlike which prevails to the very end of their lives.

They are so laughing, and so merry, all these little Nipponese dolls! Rather a forced mirth, it is true, studied, and at times with a false ring; nevertheless one is attracted by it.

Chrysantheme is an exception, for she is melancholy. What thoughts are running through that little brain? My knowledge of her language is still too limited to enable me to find out. Moreover, it is a hundred to one that she has no thoughts whatever. And even if she had, what do I care?

I have chosen her to amuse me, and I should really prefer that she should have one of those insignificant little thoughtless faces like all the others.

VIII

THE NECESSARY VEIL

When night comes on, we light two hanging lamps of religious symbolism, which burn till daylight, before our gilded idol.

We sleep on the floor, on a thin cotton mattress, which is unfolded and laid out over our white matting. Chrysantheme's pillow is a little wooden block, cut so as to fit exactly the nape of her neck, without disturbing the elaborate head-dress, which must never be taken down; the pretty black hair I shall probably never see undone. My pillow, a Chinese model, is a kind of little square drum covered over with serpent- skin.

We sleep under a gauze mosquito-net of sombre greenish-blue, dark as the shades of night, stretched out on an orange-colored ribbon. (These are the traditional colors, and all respectable families of Nagasaki possess a similar net.) It envelops us like a tent; the mosquitoes and the night- moths whirl around it.

This sounds very pretty, and written down looks very well. In reality, however, it is not so; something, I know not what, is lacking, and everything is very paltry. In other lands, in the delightful isles of Oceania, in the old, lifeless quarters of Stamboul, it seemed as if mere words could never express all I felt, and I struggled vainly against my own inability to render, in human language, the penetrating charm surrounding me.

Here, on the contrary, words exact and truthful in themselves seem always too thrilling, too great for the subject; seem to embellish it unduly. I feel as if I were acting, for my own benefit, some wretchedly trivial and third-rate comedy; and whenever I try to consider my home in a serious spirit, the scoffing figure of M. Kangourou rises before me— the matrimonial agent, to whom I am indebted for my happiness.

IX

MY PLAYTHING

July 12th.

Yves visits us whenever he is free, in the evening at five o'clock, after his duties on board are fulfilled.

He is our only European visitor, and, with the exception of a few civilities and cups of tea, exchanged with our neighbors, we lead a very retired life. Only in the evenings, winding our way through the steep, narrow streets and carrying our lanterns at the end of short sticks, we go down to Nagasaki in search of amusement at the theatres, at the tea- houses, or in the bazaars.

Yves treats my wife as if she were a plaything, and continually assures me that she is charming.

I find her as exasperating as the cicalas on my roof; and when I am alone at home, side by side with this little creature twanging the strings of her long-necked guitar, facing this marvellous panorama of pagodas and mountains, I am overcome by sadness almost to tears.

X

NOCTURNAL TERRORS

July 13th.

Last night, as we reposed under the Japanese roof of Diou-djen-dji—the thin old wooden roof scorched by a hundred years of sunshine, vibrating at the least sound, like the stretched-out parchment of a tomtom—in the silence which prevails at two o'clock in the morning, we heard overhead a sound like a regular wild huntsman's chase passing at full gallop.

"Nidzoumi![1]" ("The mice!") said Chrysantheme.

Suddenly the word brings back to my mind yet another phrase, spoken in a very different language, in a

---

[1] Nezumi, actually this word means mice and also rat (Editor footnote).

country far away from here: "Setchan!" a word heard elsewhere, a word that has likewise been whispered in my ear by a woman's voice, under similar circumstances, in a moment of nocturnal terror—"Setchan!" It was during one of our first nights at Stamboul spent under the mysterious roof of Eyoub, when danger surrounded us on all sides; a noise on the steps of the black staircase had made us tremble, and she also, my dear little Turkish companion[1], had said to me in her beloved language, "Setchan!" ("the mice!").

At that fond recollection, a thrill of sweet memories coursed through my veins; it was as if I had been startled out of a long ten years' sleep; I looked down upon the doll beside me with a sort of hatred, wondering why I was there, and I arose, with almost a feeling of remorse, to escape from that blue gauze net.

I stepped out upon the veranda, and there I paused, gazing into the depths of the starlit night. Beneath me Nagasaki lay asleep, wrapped in a soft, light slumber, hushed by the murmuring sound of a thousand insects in the moonlight, and fairy-like with its roseate hues. Then, turning my head, I saw behind me the gilded idol with our lamps burning in front of it; the idol smiling the impassive smile of Buddha; and its presence seemed to cast around it something, I know not what, strange and incomprehensible. Never until now had I slept under the eye of such a god.

In the midst of the calm and silence of the night, I strove to recall my poignant impressions of Stamboul; but, alas, I strove in vain, they would not return to me in this strange, far-off world. Through the transparent blue

---

[1] See the novel Aziyadé *(Editor footnote).*

gauze appeared my little Japanese, as she lay in her sombre night- robe with all the fantastic grace of her country, the nape of her neck resting on its wooden block, and her hair arranged in large, shiny bows. Her amber-tinted arms, pretty and delicate, emerged, bare up to the shoulders, from her wide sleeves.

"What can those mice on the roof have done to him?" thought Chrysantheme. Of course she could not understand. In a coaxing manner, like a playful kitten, she glanced at me with her half-closed eyes, inquiring why I did not come back to sleep—and I returned to my place by her side.

XI

July 14th.

This is the National Fete day of France. In Nagasaki Harbor, all the ships are adorned with flags, and salutes are fired in our honor.

Alas! All day long, I can not help thinking of that last fourteenth of July, spent in the deep calm and quiet of my old home, the door shut against all intruders, while the gay crowd roared outside; there I had remained till evening, seated on a bench, shaded by an arbor covered with honeysuckle, where, in the bygone days of my childhood's summers, I used to settle myself with my copybooks and pretend to learn my lessons. Oh, those days when I was supposed to learn my lessons! How my thoughts used to rove—what voyages, what distant lands, what tropical forests did I not behold in my dreams! At that time, near the garden-bench, in some of the crevices in the stone wall, dwelt many a big, ugly, black spider always on the alert, peeping out of his nook ready to pounce upon any giddy fly or wandering centipede. One of my amusements consisted in tickling the spiders gently, very gently, with a blade of grass or a cherry-stalk in their webs. Mystified, they would rush out, fancying they had to deal with some sort of prey, while I would rapidly draw back my hand in disgust. Well, last year, on that fourteenth of July, as I recalled my days of Latin themes and translations, now forever flown, and this game of boyish days, I actually recognized the very same spiders (or at least their daughters), lying in wait in the very same places. Gazing at them, and at the tufts of grass and moss around me, a thousand memories of those summers of my early life welled up within me, memories which for years past had lain slumbering under this old wall, sheltered by the ivy boughs. While all that is ourselves perpetually changes and passes away, the constancy with which Nature repeats, always in the same manner, her most infinitesimal details, seems a wonderful mystery; the same peculiar species of moss grows afresh for centuries on precisely the same spot, and the same little insects each summer do the same thing in the same place.

I must admit that this episode of my childhood, and the spiders, have little to do with the story of Chrysantheme. But an incongruous interruption is quite in keeping with the taste of this country; everywhere it is practised, in conversation, in music, even in painting; a landscape painter, for instance, when he has finished a picture of mountains and crags, will not hesitate to draw, in the very middle of the sky, a circle, or a lozenge, or some kind of framework, within which he will represent anything incoherent and inappropriate: a bonze fanning himself, or a lady taking a cup of tea. Nothing is more thoroughly Japanese than such digressions, made without the slightest apropos.

Moreover, if I roused my past memories, it was the better to force myself to notice the difference between that day of July last year, so peacefully spent amid surroundings familiar to me from my earliest infancy, and my present animated life passed in the midst of such a novel world.

To-day, therefore, under the scorching midday sun, at two o'clock, three swift-footed djins dragged us at full speed—Yves, Chrysantheme, and myself—in Indian file, each in a little jolting cart, to the farther end of Nagasaki, and there deposited us at the foot of some gigantic steps that run straight up the mountain.

These are the granite steps leading to the great temple of Osueva, wide enough to give access to a whole regiment; they are as grand and imposing as any work of Babylon or Nineveh, and in complete contrast with all the finical surroundings.

We climb up and up—Chrysantheme listlessly, affecting fatigue, under her paper parasol painted with pink butterflies on a black ground. As we ascended, we passed under enormous monastic porticoes, also in granite of rude and primitive style. In truth, these steps and these temple porticoes are the only imposing works that this people has created, and they astonish, for they do not seem Japanese.

We climb still higher. At this sultry hour of the day, from top to bottom of the enormous gray steps, only we three are to be seen; on all that granite there are but the pink butterflies on Chrysantheme's parasol to give a cheerful and brilliant touch.

We passed through the first temple yard, in which are two white china turrets, bronze lanterns, and the statue of a large horse in jade. Then, without pausing at the sanctuary, we turned to the left, and entered a shady garden, which formed a terrace halfway up the hill, at the extremity of which was situated the Donko-Tchaya—in English, the Teahouse of the Toads.

This was the place where Chrysantheme had wished to take us. We sat down at a table, under a black linen tent decorated with large white letters (of funereal aspect), and two laughing 'mousmes' hastened to wait upon us.

The word 'mousme' means a young girl, or very young woman. It is one of the prettiest words in the Nipponese language; it seems almost as if there were a little pout in the very sound—a pretty, taking little pout, such as they put on, and also as if a little pert physiognomy were described by it. I shall often make use of it, knowing none other in our own language that conveys the same meaning.

Some Japanese Watteau must have mapped out this Donko-Tchaya, for it has rather an affected air of rurality, though very pretty. It is well shaded, under a shelter of large trees with dense foliage, and a miniature lake close by, the chosen residence of a few toads, has given it its attractive denomination. Lucky toads, who crawl and croak on the finest of moss, in the midst of tiny artificial islets decked with gardenias in full bloom. From time to time, one of them informs us of his thoughts by a 'Couac', uttered in a deep bass croak, infinitely more hollow than that of our own toads.

Under the tent of this tea-house, we sit on a sort of balcony jutting out from the mountain-side, overhanging from on high the grayish town and its suburbs buried in greenery. Around, above, and beneath us cling and hang, on every possible point, clumps of trees and fresh green woods, with the delicate and varying foliage of the temperate zone. We can see, at our feet, the deep roadstead, foreshortened and slanting, diminished in appearance till it looks like a sombre rent in the mass of large green mountains; and farther still, quite low on the black and stagnant waters, are the men-of-war, the steamboats and the junks, with flags flying from every mast. Against the dark green, which is the dominant shade everywhere, stand out these thousand scraps of bunting, emblems of the different nationalities, all displayed, all flying in honor of far- distant France. The colors most prevailing in this motley assemblage are the white flag with a red ball, emblem of the Empire of the Rising Sun, where we now are.

With the exception of three or four 'mousmes' at the farther end, who are practising with bows and arrows[1], we are today the only people in the garden, and the mountain round about is silent.

Having finished her cigarette and her cup of tea, Chrysantheme also wishes to exert her skill; for archery is still held in honor among the young women.

The old man who keeps the range picks out for her his best arrows tipped with white and red feathers—and she takes aim with a serious air. The mark is a circle, traced in the middle of a picture on which is painted, in flat, gray tones, terrifying chimera flying through the clouds.

Chrysantheme is certainly an adroit markswoman, and we admire her as much as she expected.

---

[1] Probably Kyudo, a martial art *(Editor footnote)*.

Then Yves, who is usually clever at all games of skill, wishes to try his luck, and fails. It is amusing to see her, with her mincing ways and smiles, arrange with the tips of her little fingers the sailor's broad hands, placing them on the bow and the string in order to teach him the proper manner. Never have they seemed to get on so well together, Yves and my doll, and I might even feel anxious, were I less sure of my good brother, and if, moreover, it was not a matter of perfect indifference to me.

In the stillness of the garden, amid the balmy peacefulness of these mountains, a loud noise suddenly startles us; a unique, powerful, terrible sound, which is prolonged in infinite metallic vibrations. It begins again, sounding more appalling: 'Boum!' borne to us by the rising wind.

"Nippon Kane!" exclaims Chrysantheme—and she again takes up her brightly feathered arrows. "Nippon Kane ("the Japanese brass"); it is the Japanese brass that is sounding!" It is the monstrous gong of a monastery, situated in a suburb beneath us. It is powerful indeed, "the Japanese brass"! When the strokes are ended, when it is no longer heard, a vibration seems to linger among the suspended foliage, and a prolonged quiver runs through the air.

I am obliged to admit that Chrysantheme looks very charming shooting her arrows, her figure well bent back the better to bend her bow; her loose- hanging sleeves caught up to her shoulders, showing the graceful bare arms polished like amber and very much the same color. Each arrow whistles by with the rustle of a bird's wing— then a short, sharp little blow is heard, the target is hit, always.

At nightfall, when Chrysantheme has gone up to Diou-djen-dji, we cross, Yves and I, the European concession, on our way to the ship, to take up our watch till the following day. The cosmopolitan quarter, exhaling an odor of absinthe, is dressed up with flags, and squibs are being fired off in honor of France. Long lines of djins pass by, dragging, as fast as their naked legs can carry them, the crew of the 'Triomphante,' who are shouting and fanning themselves. The Marseillaise is heard everywhere; English sailors are singing it, gutturally, with a dull and slow cadence like their own "God Save." In all the American bars, grinding organs are hammering it with many an odious variation and flourish, in order to attract our men.

One amusing recollection comes back to me of that evening. On our return, we had by mistake turned into a street inhabited by a multitude of ladies of doubtful reputation. I can still see that big fellow Yves, struggling with a whole band of tiny little 'mousmes' of twelve or fifteen years of age, who barely reached up to his waist, and were pulling him by the sleeves, eager to lead him astray. Astonished and indignant, he repeated, as he extricated himself from their clutches, "Oh, this is too much!" so shocked was he at seeing such mere babies, so young, so tiny, already so brazen and shameless.

XII

HAPPY FAMILIES !

July 18th.

By this time, four officers of my ship are married like myself, and inhabiting the slopes of the same suburb. This arrangement is quite an ordinary occurrence, and is brought about without difficulties, mystery, or danger, through the offices of the same M. Kangourou.

As a matter of course, we are on visiting terms with all these ladies.

First, there is our very merry neighbor Madame Campanule, who is little Charles N*'s wife; then Madame Jonquille, who is even merrier than Campanule, like a young bird, and the daintiest fairy of them all; she has married X*, a fair northerner who adores her; they are a lover- like and inseparable pair, the only one that will probably weep when the hour of parting comes. Then Sikou-San with Doctor Y*; and lastly the midshipman Z* with the tiny Madame Touki-San, no taller than a boot: thirteen years old at the outside, and already a regular woman, full of her own importance, a petulant little gossip. In my childhood I was sometimes taken to the Learned Animals Theatre, and I remember a certain Madame de Pompadour, a principal role, filled by a gayly dressed old monkey; Touki-San reminds me of her.

In the evening, all these folk usually come and fetch us for a long processional walk with lighted lanterns. My wife, more serious, more melancholy, perhaps even more refined, and belonging, I fancy, to a higher class, tries when these friends come to us to play the part of the lady of the house. It is comical to see the entry of these ill-matched pairs, partners for a day, the ladies, with their disjointed bows, falling on all fours before Chrysantheme, the queen of the establishment. When we are all assembled, we set out, arm in arm, one behind another, and always carrying at the end of our short sticks little white or red paper lanterns; it is a pretty custom.

We are obliged to scramble down the kind of street, or rather goat's- path, which leads to the Japanese Nagasaki — with the prospect, alas! of having to climb up again at night; clamber up all the steps, all the slippery slopes, stumble over all the stones, before we shall be able to get home, go to bed, and sleep. We make our descent in the darkness, under the branches, under the foliage, among dark gardens and venerable little houses that throw but a faint glimmer on the road; and when the moon is absent or clouded over, our lanterns are by no means unnecessary.

When at last we reach the bottom, suddenly, without transition, we find ourselves in the very heart of Nagasaki and its busy throng in a long illuminated street, where vociferating djins hurry along and thousands of paper lanterns swing and gleam in the wind. It is life and animation, after the peace of our silent suburb.

Here, decorum requires that we should separate from our wives. All five take hold of each others' hands, like a batch of little girls out walking. We follow them with an air of indifference. Seen from behind, our dolls are really very dainty, with their back hair so tidily arranged, their tortoiseshell pins so coquettishly placed. They shuffle along, their high wooden clogs making an ugly sound, striving to walk with their toes turned in, according to the height of fashion and elegance. At every minute they burst out laughing.

Yes, seen from behind, they are very pretty; they have, like all Japanese women, the most lovely turn of the head. Moreover, they are very funny, thus drawn up in line. In speaking of them, we say: "Our little trained dogs," and in truth they are singularly like them.

This great Nagasaki is the same from one end to another, with its numberless petroleum lamps burning, its many-colored lanterns flickering, and innumerable panting djins. Always the same narrow streets, lined on each side with the same low houses, built of paper and wood. Always the same shops, without glass windows, open to all the winds, equally rudimentary, whatever may be sold or made in them; whether they display the finest gold lacquer ware, the most marvellous china jars, or old worn-out pots and pans, dried fish, and ragged frippery. All the salesmen are seated on the ground in the midst of their valuable or trumpery merchandise, their legs bared nearly to the waist.

And all kinds of queer little trades are carried on under the public gaze, by strangely primitive means, by workmen of the most ingenious type.

Oh, what wonderful goods are exposed for sale in those streets! What whimsical extravagance in those bazaars!

No horses, no carriages are ever seen in the town; nothing but people on foot, or the comical little carts dragged along by the runners. Some few Europeans straggling hither and thither, wanderers from the ships in harbor; some Japanese (fortunately as yet but few) dressed up in coats; other natives who content themselves with adding to their national costume the pot-hat, from which their long, sleek locks hang down; and all around, eager haggling, bargaining, and laughter.

In the bazaars every evening our mousmes make endless purchases; like spoiled children they buy everything they fancy: toys, pins, ribbons, flowers. And then they prettily offer one another presents, with childish little smiles. For instance, Campanule buys for Chrysantheme an ingeniously contrived lantern on which, set in motion by some invisible machinery, Chinese shadows dance in a ring round the flame. In return, Chrysantheme gives Campanule a magic fan, with paintings that change at will from butterflies fluttering around cherry-blossoms to outlandish monsters pursuing each other across black clouds. Touki offers Sikou a cardboard mask representing the bloated countenance of Dai-Cok, god of wealth; and Sikou replies with a present of a long crystal trumpet, by means of which are produced the most extraordinary sounds, like a turkey gobbling. Everything is uncouth, fantastical to excess, grotesquely lugubrious; everywhere we are surprised by incomprehensible conceptions, which seem the work of distorted imaginations.

In the fashionable tea-houses, where we finish our evenings, the little serving-maids now bow to us, on our arrival, with an air of respectful recognition, as belonging to the fast set of Nagasaki. There we carry on desultory conversations, full of misunderstandings and endless 'quid pro quo' of uncouth words, in little gardens lighted up with lanterns, near ponds full of goldfish, with little bridges, little islets, and little ruined towers. They hand us tea and white and pink-colored sweetmeats flavored with pepper that taste strange and unfamiliar, and beverages mixed with snow tasting of flowers or perfumes.

To give a faithful account of those evenings would require a more affected style than our own; and some kind of graphic sign would have also to be expressly invented and scattered at haphazard among the words, indicating the moment when the reader should laugh — rather a forced laugh, perhaps, but amiable and gracious. The evening at an end, it is time to return up there.

Oh! that street, that road, that we must clamber up every evening, under the starlit sky or the heavy thunder-clouds, dragging by the hands our drowsy mousmes in order to regain our homes perched on high halfway up the hill, where our bed of matting awaits us.

XIII

OUR "VERY TALL FRIEND"

The cleverest among us has been Louis de S*. Having formerly inhabited Japan, and made a marriage Japanese fashion there, he is now satisfied to remain the friend of our wives, of whom he has become the 'Komodachi taksan takai' ("the very tall friend," as they say, on account of his excessive height and slenderness). Speaking Japanese more readily than we, he is their confidential adviser, disturbs or reconciles our households at will, and has infinite amusement at our expense.

This "very tall friend" of our wives enjoys all the fun that these little creatures can give him, without any of the worries of domestic life. With brother Yves, and little Oyouki (the daughter of Madame Prune, my landlady), he makes up our incongruous party.

XIV

OUR PIOUS HOSTS

M. Sucre and Madame Prune, my landlord and his wife, two perfectly unique personages recently escaped from the panel of some screen, live below us on the ground floor; and very old they seem to have this daughter of fifteen, Oyouki, who is Chrysantheme's inseparable friend.

Both of them are entirely absorbed in the practices of Shinto religion: perpetually on their knees before their family altar, perpetually occupied in murmuring their lengthy orisons to the spirits, and clapping their hands from time to time to recall around them the inattentive essences floating in the atmosphere. In their spare moments they cultivate, in little pots of gayly painted earthenware, dwarf shrubs and unheard-of flowers which are delightfully fragrant in the evening.

M. Sucre is taciturn, dislikes society, and looks like a mummy in his blue cotton dress. He writes a great deal (his memoirs, I fancy), with a paint-brush held in his fingertips, on long strips of rice-paper of a faint gray tint.

Madame Prune is eagerly attentive, obsequious, and rapacious; her eyebrows are closely shaven, her teeth carefully lacquered with black, as befits a lady of gentility, and at all and no matter what hours, she appears on all fours at the entrance of our apartment, to offer us her services.

As to Oyouki, she rushes upon us ten times a day— whether we are sleeping or dressing—like a whirlwind on a visit, flashing upon us, a very gust of dainty youthfulness and droll gayety—a living peal of laughter. She is round of figure, round of face; half baby, half girl; and so affectionate that she bestows kisses on the slightest occasion with her great puffy lips—a little moist, it is true, like a child's, but nevertheless very fresh and very red.

XV

Our dwelling is open all the night through, and the lamps burning before the gilded Buddha bring us the company of the insect inhabitants of every garden in the neighborhood. Moths, mosquitoes, cicalas, and other extraordinary insects of which I don't even know the names—all this company assembles around us.

It is extremely funny, when some unexpected grasshopper, some free-and- easy beetle presents itself without invitation or excuse, scampering over our white mats, to see the manner in which Chrysantheme indicates it to my righteous vengeance—merely pointing her finger at it, without another word than "Hou!" said with bent head, a particular pout, and a scandalised air.

There is a fan kept expressly for the purpose of blowing them out of doors again.

XVI

SLEEPING JAPAN

Here I must own that my story must appear to the reader to drag a little.

Lacking exciting intrigues and tragic adventures, I wish I knew how to infuse into it a little of the sweet perfumes of the gardens which surround me, something of the gentle warmth of the sunshine, of the shade of these graceful trees. Love being wanting, I should like it to breathe of the restful tranquillity of this faraway spot. Then, too, I should like it to reecho the sound of Chrysantheme's guitar, in which I begin to find a certain charm, for want of something better, in the silence of the lovely summer evenings.

All through these moonlit nights of July, the weather has been calm, luminous, and magnificent. Ah, what glorious clear nights! What exquisite roseate tints beneath that wonderful moon, what mystery of blue shadows in the thick tangle of trees! And, from the heights where stood our veranda, how prettily the town lay sleeping at our feet!

After all, I do not positively detest this little Chrysantheme, and when there is no repugnance on either side, habit turns into a makeshift of attachment.

XVII

THE SONG OF THE CICALA

Forever, throughout everything, rises day and night from the whole country the song of the cicalas, ceaseless, strident, and insistent. It is everywhere, and never-ending, at no matter what hour of the burning day, or what hour of the refreshing night. From the harbor, as we approached our anchorage, we had heard it at the same time from both shores, from both walls of green mountains. It is wearisome and haunting; it seems to be the manifestation, the noise expressive of the kind of life peculiar to this region of the world. It is the voice of summer in these islands; it is the song of unconscious rejoicing, always content with itself and always appearing to inflate, to rise, in a greater and greater exultation at the sheer happiness of living.

It is to me the noise characteristic of this country—this, and the cry of the falcon, which had in like manner greeted our entry into Japan. Over the valleys and the deep bay sail these birds, uttering, from time to time, their three cries, "Ha! ha! ha!" in a key of sadness that seems the extreme of painful astonishment. And the mountains around reecho their cry.

XVIII

MY FRIEND AND MY DOLL

Chrysantheme, Yves, and little Oyouki have struck up a friendship so intimate that it amuses me. I even think that in my home life this intimacy is what affords me the greatest entertainment. They form a contrast which gives rise to the most absurd jokes, and unexpected situations. He brings into this fragile little paper house his nautical freedom and ease of manner, and his Breton accent; and these tiny mousmes, with affected manners and bird-like voices, small as they are, rule the big fellow as they please; make him eat with chop-sticks; teach him Japanese pigeon-vole, cheat him, and quarrel, and almost die of laughter over it all.

Certainly he and Chrysantheme take a pleasure in each other's society. But I remain serenely undisturbed, and can not imagine that this little doll, with whom I play at married life, could possibly occasion any serious trouble between this "brother" and me.

XIX

MY JAPANESE RELATIVES

Japanese relatives, very numerous and conspicuous, are a great source of amusement to those of my brother officers who visit me in my villa on the hill—most especially to 'komodachi taksan takaï'[1] ("the tall friend").

I have a charming mother-in-law—quite a woman of the world—tiny sisters -in-law, little cousins, and aunts who are still quite young.

I have even a poor second cousin, who is a djin. There was some hesitation in owning this latter to me; but, behold! during the ceremony of introduction, we exchanged a smile of recognition. It was Number 415!

Over this poor Number 415 my friends on board crack no end of jokes—one in particular, who, less than any one has the right to make them, little Charles N——, for his mother-in-law was once a concierge, or something of the kind, at the gateway of a pagoda.

I, however, who have a great respect for strength and agility, much appreciate this new relative of mine. His legs are undoubtedly the best in all Nagasaki, and whenever I am in haste, I always beg Madame Prune to send down to the djin-stand and engage my cousin.

---

[1] « Tomodachi takusan takaï » *(Editor footnote).*

XX

A DEAD FAIRY

Today I arrived unexpectedly at Diou-djen-dji, in the midst of burning noonday heat. At the foot of the stairs lay Chrysantheme's wooden shoes and her sandals of varnished leather.

In our rooms, upstairs, all was open to the air, bamboo blinds hung on the sunny side, and through their transparency came warm air and golden threads of light. Today the flowers Chrysantheme had placed in the bronze vases were lotus, and as I entered, my eyes fell upon their wide rosy cups.

According to her usual custom, Chrysantheme was lying flat on the floor enjoying her daily siesta.

What a singular originality these bouquets of Chrysantheme always have: a something, difficult to define, a Japanese slightness, an artificial grace which we never should succeed in imparting to them.

She was sleeping, face down, upon the mats, her high headdress and tortoise-shell pins standing out boldly from the rest of the horizontal figure. The train of her tunic appeared to prolong her delicate little body, like the tail of a bird; her arms were stretched crosswise, the sleeves spread out like wings, and her long guitar lay beside her.

She looked like a dead fairy; still more did she resemble some great blue dragon-fly, which, having alighted on that spot, some unkind hand had pinned to the floor.

Madame Prune, who had come upstairs after me, always officious and eager, manifested by her gestures her sentiments of indignation on beholding the careless reception accorded by Chrysantheme to her lord and master, and advanced to wake her.

"Pray do nothing of the kind, my good Madame Prune; you don't know how much I prefer her like that!" I had left my shoes below, according to custom, beside the little shoes and sandals; and I entered on the tips of my toes, very, very, softly to sit awhile on the veranda.

What a pity this little Chrysantheme can not always be asleep; she is really extremely decorative seen in this manner—and like this, at least, she does not bore me. Who knows what may be passing in that little head and heart! If I only had the means of finding out! But strange to say, since we have kept house together, instead of advancing in my study of the Japanese language, I have neglected it, so much have I felt the impossibility of ever interesting myself in the subject.

Seated upon my veranda, my eyes wandered over the temples and cemeteries spread at my feet, over the woods and the green mountains, over Nagasaki lying bathed in the sunlight. The cicalas were chirping their loudest, the strident noise trembling feverishly in the hot air. All was calm, full of light and full of heat.

Nevertheless, to my taste, it is not yet enough so! What, then, can have changed upon the earth? The burning noondays of summer, such as I can recall in days gone by, were more brilliant, more full of sunshine; Nature seemed to me in those days more powerful, more terrible. One would say this was only a pale copy of all that I knew in early years— a copy in which something is wanting. Sadly do I ask myself—Is the splendor of the summer only this? Was it only this? or is it the fault of my eyes, and as time goes on shall I behold everything around me fading still more?

Behind me comes a faint and melancholy strain of music—melancholy enough to make one shiver—and shrill, shrill as the song of the grasshoppers, it began to make itself heard, very softly at first, then growing louder and rising in the silence of the noonday like the diminutive wail of some poor Japanese soul in pain and anguish; it was Chrysantheme and her guitar awaking together.

It pleased me that the idea should have occurred to her to greet me with music, instead of eagerly hastening to wish me good-morning. At no time have I ever given myself the trouble to pretend the slightest affection for her, and a certain coldness even has grown up between us, especially when we are alone. But to-day I turn to her with a smile, and wave my hand for her to continue. "Go on, it amuses me to listen to your quaint little impromptu." It is singular that the music of this essentially merry people should be so plaintive. But undoubtedly that which Chrysantheme is playing at this moment is worth listening to. Whence can it have come to her? What unutterable dreams, forever hidden from me, surge beneath her ivory brow, when she plays or sings in this manner?

Suddenly I hear some one tapping three times, with a harsh and bony finger, against one of the steps of our stairs, and in our doorway appears an idiot, clad in a suit of gray tweed, who bows low. "Come in, come in, Monsieur Kangourou. You come just in the nick of time! I was actually becoming enthusiastic over your country!"

M. Kangourou brought a little laundry bill, which he wished respectfully to hand to me, with a profound bend of the whole body, the correct pose of the hands on the knees, and a long, snake-like hiss.

XXI

ANCIENT TOMBS

Pursuing the path that winds past our, dwelling, one passes a dozen or more old villas, a few garden-walls, and then sees nothing but the lonely mountain-side, with little paths winding upward toward the summit through plantations of tea, bushes of camellias, underbrush, and rocks. The mountains round Nagasaki are covered with cemeteries; for centuries and centuries they have brought their dead up here.

But there is neither sadness nor horror in these Japanese sepulchres; it seems as if, among this frivolous and childish people, death itself could not be taken seriously. The monuments are either granite Buddhas, seated on lotus, or upright tombstones with inscriptions in gold. They are grouped together in little enclosures in the midst of the woods, or on natural terraces delightfully situated, and are usually reached by long stairways of stone carpeted with moss. Sometimes these pass under one of the sacred gateways, of which the shape, always the same, rude and simple, is a smaller reproduction of those in the temples.

Above us, the tombs of our mountain are of an antiquity so hoary that they no longer alarm any one, even at night. It is a region of forsaken cemeteries. The dead hidden away there have long since become one with the earth around them; and these thousands of little gray stones, these multitudes of ancient little Buddhas, eaten away by lichens, seem to be now no more than a proof of a series of existences, long anterior to our own, and lost forever and altogether in the mysterious depths of ages.

Pursuing the path that winds past our, dwelling, one passes a dozen or more old villas, a few garden-walls, and then sees nothing but the lonely mountain-side, with little paths winding upward toward the summit through plantations of tea, bushes of camellias, underbrush, and rocks. The mountains round Nagasaki are covered with cemeteries; for centuries and centuries they have brought their dead up here.

But there is neither sadness nor horror in these Japanese sepulchres; it seems as if, among this frivolous and childish people, death itself could not be taken seriously. The monuments are either granite Buddhas, seated on lotus, or upright tombstones with inscriptions in gold. They are grouped together in little enclosures in the midst of the woods, or on natural terraces delightfully situated, and are usually reached by long stairways of stone carpeted with moss. Sometimes these pass under one of the sacred gateways, of which the shape, always the same, rude and simple, is a smaller reproduction of those in the temples.

Above us, the tombs of our mountain are of an antiquity so hoary that they no longer alarm any one, even at night. It is a region of forsaken cemeteries. The dead hidden away there have long since become one with the earth around them; and these thousands of little gray stones, these multitudes of ancient little Buddhas, eaten away by lichens, seem to be now no more than a proof of a series of existences, long anterior to our own, and lost forever and altogether in the mysterious depths of ages.

CHAPTER XXII

DAINTY DISHES FOR A DOLL

The meals that Chrysantheme enjoys are something almost indescribable.

She begins in the morning, when she wakes, with two little green wild plums pickled in vinegar and rolled in powdered sugar. A cup of tea completes this almost traditional breakfast of Japan, the very same that Madame Prune is eating downstairs, the same that is served in the inns to travellers.

At intervals during the day the meals are continued by two little dinners of the drollest description. They are brought up on a tray of red lacquer, in microscopic cups with covers, from Madame Prune's apartment, where they are cooked: a hashed sparrow, a stuffed prawn, seaweed with a sauce, a salted sweetmeat, a sugared chili! Chrysantheme tastes a little of all, with dainty pecks and the aid of her little chopsticks, raising the tips of her fingers with affected grace. At every dish she makes a face, leaves three parts of it, and dries her finger-tips after it in apparent disgust.

These menus vary according to the inspiration that may have seized Madame Prune. But one thing never varies, either in our household or in any other, neither in the north nor in the south of the Empire, and that is the dessert and the manner of eating it: after all these little dishes, which are a mere make-believe, a wooden bowl is brought in, bound with copper—an enormous bowl, fit for Gargantua, and filled to the very brim with rice, plainly cooked in water. Chrysantheme fills another large bowl from it (sometimes twice, sometimes three times), darkens its snowy whiteness with a black sauce flavored with fish, which is contained in a delicately shaped blue cruet, mixes it all together, carries the bowl to her lips, and crams down all the rice, shovelling it with her two chop- sticks into her very throat. Next the little cups and covers are picked up, as well as the tiniest crumb that may have fallen upon the white mats, the irreproachable purity of which nothing is allowed to tarnish. And so ends the dinner.

CHAPTER XXIII

A FANTASTIC FUNERAL

Below, in the town, a street-singer had established herself in a little thoroughfare; people had gathered around her to listen to her singing, and we three—that is, Yves, Chrysantheme, and I—who happened to be passing, stopped also.

She was quite young, rather fat, and fairly pretty, and she strummed her guitar and sang, rolling her eyes fiercely, like a virtuoso executing feats of difficulty. She lowered her head, stuck her chin into her neck, in order to draw deeper notes from the furthermost recesses of her body; and succeeded in bringing forth a great, hoarse voice—a voice that might have belonged to an aged frog, a ventriloquist's voice, coming whence it would be impossible to say (this is the best stage manner, the last touch of art, in the interpretation of tragic pieces).

Yves cast an indignant glance upon her.

"Good gracious," said he, "she has the voice of a …" (words failed him, in his astonishment) "the voice of a … a monster!"

And he looked at me, almost frightened by this little being, and desirous to know what I thought of it.

Yves was out of temper on this occasion, because I had induced him to come out in a straw hat with a turned-up brim, which did not please him.

"That hat suits you remarkably well, Yves, I assure you," I said.

"Oh, indeed! You say so, you. For my part, I think it looks like a magpie's nest!"

As a fortunate diversion from the singer and the hat, here comes a cortege, advancing toward us from the end of the street, something remarkably like a funeral. Bonzes march in front, dressed in robes of black gauze, having much the appearance of Catholic priests; the principal object of interest of the procession, the corpse, comes last, laid in a sort of little closed palanquin, which is daintily pretty. This is followed by a band of mousmes, hiding their laughing faces beneath a kind of veil, and carrying in vases of the sacred shape the artificial lotus with silver petals indispensable at a funeral; then come fine ladies, on foot, smirking and stifling a wish to laugh, beneath parasols on which are painted, in the gayest colors, butterflies and storks.

Now they are quite close to us, we must stand back to give them room. Chrysantheme all at once assumes a suitable air of gravity, and Yves bares his head, taking off the magpie's nest.

Yes, it is true, it is death that is passing!

I had almost lost sight of the fact, so little does this procession recall it.

The procession will climb high above Nagasaki, into the heart of the green mountain covered with tombs. There the poor fellow will be laid at rest, with his palanquin above him, and his vases and his flowers of silvered paper. Well, at least he will lie in a charming spot commanding a lovely view.

Then they will return half laughing, half snivelling, and tomorrow no one will think of it again.

CHAPTER XXIV

SOCIABILITY

August 4th.

Our ship, the 'Triomphante', which has been lying in the harbor almost at the foot of the hill on which stands my house, enters the dock to-day to undergo repairs rendered necessary by the long blockade of Formosa[1].

I am now a long way from my home, and am compelled to cross by boat the whole breadth of the bay when I wish to see Chrysantheme; for the dock is situated on the shore, opposite to Diou-djen-dji. It is sunk in a little valley, narrow and deep, midst all kinds of foliage— bamboos, camellias, trees of all sorts; our masts and spars, seen from the deck, look as if they were tangled among the branches.

The situation of the vessel—no longer afloat—gives the crew a greater facility for clandestine escapes from the ship at no matter what hour of the night, and our sailors have made friends with all the girls of the villages perched on the mountains above us.

These quarters, and this excessive liberty, give me some uneasiness about my poor Yves; for this country of frivolous pleasure has a little turned his head.

---

[1] France and China were in war *(Editor footnote).*

Moreover, I am more and more convinced that he is in love with Chrysantheme.

It is really a pity that the sentiment has not occurred to me instead, since it is I who have gone the length of marrying her.

CHAPTER XXV

UNWELCOME GUESTS

Despite the increased distance, I continue my regular visits to Diou- djen-dji. When night has fallen, and the four couples who compose our society have joined us, as well as Yves and the "amazingly tall friend"— we descend again into the town, stumbling by lantern-light down the steep stairways and slopes of the old suburb.

This nocturnal ramble is always the same, and is accompanied always by the same amusements: we pause before the same queer booths, we drink the same sugared drinks served to us in the same little gardens. But our troop is often more numerous: to begin with, we chaperon Oyouki, who is confided to our care by her parents; then we have two cousins of my wife's—pretty little creatures; and lastly friends—guests of sometimes only ten or twelve years old, little girls of the neighborhood to whom our mousmes wish to show some politeness.

Thus a singular company of tiny beings forms our suite and follows us into the tea-gardens in the evenings! The most absurd faces, with sprigs of flowers stuck in the oddest fashion in their comical and childish heads. One might suppose it was a whole school of mousmes out for an evening's frolic under our care.

Yves returns with us, when the time comes to remount our hill; Chrysantheme heaves great sighs like a tired child, and stops on every step, leaning on our arms.

When we have reached our destination he says "Goodnight," just touches Chrysantheme's hand, and descending once more by the slope which leads to the quays and the shipping, he crosses the roadstead in a sampan, to get on board the 'Triomphante.'

Meantime, we, with the aid of a sort of secret key, open the door of our garden, where Madame Prune's pots of flowers, ranged in the darkness, send forth delicious odors in the night air. We cross the garden by moonlight or starlight, and mount to our own rooms.

If it is very late—a frequent occurrence—we find all our wooden panels drawn and tightly shut by the careful M. Sucre (as a precaution against thieves), and our apartment is as close and as private as if it were a real European house.

In this dwelling, when every chink is thus closed, a strange odor mingles with the musk and the lotus—an odor essential to Japan, to the yellow race, belonging to the soil or emanating from the venerable woodwork; almost an odor of wild beasts. The mosquito-curtain of dark-blue gauze, ready hung for the night, falls from the ceiling with the air of a mysterious vellum. The gilded Buddha smiles eternally at the night-lamps burning before him; some great moth, a constant frequenter of the house, which during the day sleeps clinging to our ceiling, flutters at this hour under the very nose of the god, turning and flitting round the thin, quivering flames. And, motionless on the wall, its feelers spread out star-like, sleeps some great garden spider, which one must not kill because it is night. "Hou!" says Chrysantheme, indignantly, pointing it out to me with levelled finger. Quick! where is the fan kept for the purpose, wherewith to hunt it out of doors?

Around us reigns a silence which is almost oppressive after all the joyous noises of the town, and all the laughter, now hushed, of our band of mousmes—a silence of the country, of some sleeping village.

CHAPTER XXVI

A QUIET SMOKE

The sound of the innumerable wooden panels, which at nightfall are pulled and shut in every Japanese house, is one of the peculiarities of the country which will remain longest imprinted on my memory. From our neighbor's houses these noises reach us one after the other, floating to us over the green gardens, more or less deadened, more or less distant.

Just below us, Madame Prune's panels move very badly, creak and make a hideous noise in their wornout grooves.

Ours are somewhat noisy too, for the old house is full of echoes, and there are at least twenty screens to run over long slides in order to close in completely the kind of open hall in which we live. Usually, it is Chrysantheme who undertakes this piece of household work, and a great deal of trouble it gives her, for she often pinches her fingers in the singular awkwardness of her too tiny hands, which never have been accustomed to do any work.

Then comes her toilette for the night. With a certain grace she lets fall the day-dress, and slips on a more simple one of blue cotton, which has the same pagoda sleeves, the same shape all but the train, and which she fastens round her waist with a sash of muslin of the same color.

The high head-dress remains untouched, it is needless to say—that is, all but the pins, which are taken out and laid beside her in a lacquer box.

Then there is the little silver pipe that must absolutely be smoked before going to sleep; this is one of the customs which most provoke me, but it has to be borne.

Chrysantheme squats like a gipsy before a certain square box, made of red wood, which contains a little tobacco-jar, a little porcelain stove full of hot embers, and finally a little bamboo pot serving at the same time as ash-tray and cuspidor. (Madame Prune's smoking-box downstairs, and every smoking-box in Japan, is exactly the same, and contains precisely the same objects, arranged in precisely the same manner; and wherever it may be, whether in the house of the rich or the poor, it always lies about somewhere on the floor.)

The word "pipe" is at once too trivial and too big to be applied to this delicate silver tube, which is perfectly straight and at the end of which, in a microscopic receptacle, is placed one pinch of golden tobacco, chopped finer than silken thread.

Two puffs, or at most three; it lasts scarcely a few seconds, and the pipe is finished. Then tap, tap, tap, tap, the little tube is struck smartly against the edge of the smoking-box to knock out the ashes, which never will fall; and this tapping, heard everywhere, in every house, at every hour of the day or night, quick and droll as the scratchings of a monkey, is in Japan one of the noises most characteristic of human life.

"Anata nominase!"[1] ("You must smoke too!") says Chrysantheme.

---

[1] The right word is 'nomimass' from the verb 'nomu', but actually, it means to drink ! Probably a mistake of the author *(Editor footnote).*

Having again filled the tiresome little pipe, she puts the silver tube to my lips with a bow. Courtesy forbids my refusal; but I find it detestably bitter.

Before laying myself down under the blue mosquito-net, I open two of the panels in the room, one on the side of the silent and deserted footpath, the other on the garden side, overlooking the terraces, so that the night air may breathe upon us, even at the risk of bringing the company of some belated cockchafer, or more giddy moth.

Our wooden house, with its thin old walls, vibrates at night like a great dry violin, and the slightest noises have a startling resonance.

Beneath the veranda are hung two little Æolian harps, which, at the least ruffle of the breeze running through their blades of grass, emit a gentle tinkling sound, like the harmonious murmur of a brook; outside, to the very farthest limits of the distance, the cicalas continue their sonorous and never-ending concert; over our heads, on the black roof, is heard passing, like a witch's sabbath, the raging battle, to the death, of cats, rats, and owls.

Presently, when in the early dawn a fresher breeze, mounting upward from the sea and the deep harbor, reaches us, Chrysantheme rises and slyly shuts the panels I have opened.

Before that, however, she will have risen at least three times to smoke: having yawned like a cat, stretched herself, twisted in every direction her little amber arms, and her graceful little hands, she sits up resolutely, with all the waking sighs and broken syllables of a child, pretty and fascinating enough; then she emerges from the gauze net, fills her little pipe, and breathes a few puffs of the bitter and unpleasant mixture.

Then comes tap, tap, tap, tap, against the box to shake out the ashes. In the silence of the night it makes quite a terrible noise, which wakes Madame Prune. This is fatal. Madame Prune is at once seized also with a longing to smoke which may not be denied; then, to the noise from above, comes an answering tap, tap, tap, tap, from below, exactly like it, exasperating and inevitable as an echo.

CHAPTER XXVII

THE PRAYERFUL MADAME PRUNE

More cheerful are the sounds of morning: the cocks crowing, the wooden panels all around the neighborhood sliding back upon their rollers; or the strange cry of some fruit-seller, patrolling our lofty suburb in the early dawn. And the grasshoppers actually seem to chirp more loudly, to celebrate the return of the sunlight.

Above all, rises to our ears from below the sound of Madame Prune's long prayers, ascending through the floor, monotonous as the song of a somnambulist, regular and soothing as the plash of a fountain. It lasts three quarters of an hour at least, it drones along, a rapid flow of words in a high nasal key; from time to time, when the inattentive spirits are not listening, it is accompanied by a clapping of dry palms, or by harsh sounds from a kind of wooden clapper made of two discs of mandragora root. It is an uninterrupted stream of prayer; its flow never ceases, and the quavering continues without stopping, like the bleating of a delirious old goat.

"After washing the hands and feet," say the sacred books, "the great God Ama-Terace-Omi-Kami[1], who is the royal power

> *of Japan, must be invoked; the manes of all*
> *the defunct emperors descended from him*
> *must also be invoked; next, the manes of all*
> *his personal ancestors, to the farthest*
> *generation; the spirits of the air and the sea;*
> *the spirits of all secret and impure places;*
> *the spirits of the tombs of the district whence*
> *you spring, etc., etc."*

"I worship and implore you," sings Madame Prune, "O Ama-Terace-Omi-Kami, royal power! Cease not to protect your faithful people, who are ready to sacrifice themselves for their country. Grant that I may become as holy as yourself, and drive from my mind all dark thoughts. I am a coward and a sinner: purge me from my cowardice and sinfulness, even as the north wind drives the dust into the sea. Wash me clean from all my iniquities, as one washes away uncleanness in the river of Kamo. Make me the richest woman in the world. I believe in your glory, which shall be spread over the whole earth, and illuminate it for ever for my happiness. Grant me the continued good health of my family, and above all, my own, who, O Ama-Terace-Omi-Kami! do worship and adore you, and only you, etc., etc."

Here follow all the emperors, all the spirits, and the interminable list of ancestors.

In her trembling old woman's falsetto, Madame Prune sings all this, without omitting anything, at a pace which almost takes away her breath.

And very strange it is to hear: at length it seems hardly a human voice; it sounds like a series of magic formulas, unwinding themselves from an inexhaustible

---

[1] *Amaterasu ōmikami* : Amaterasu great godess.
Amaterasu is the godess of the sun and ancestor of all japanese emperors *(Editor footnote).*

roller, and escaping to take flight through the air. By its very weirdness, and by the persistency of its incantation, it ends by producing in my half-awakened brain an almost religious impression.

Every day I wake to the sound of this Shintoist litany chanted beneath me, vibrating through the exquisite clearness of the summer mornings— while our night-lamps burn low before the smiling Buddha, while the eternal sun, hardly risen, already sends through the cracks of our wooden panels its bright rays, which dart like golden arrows through our darkened dwelling and our blue gauze tent.

This is the moment at which I must rise, descend hurriedly to the sea by grassy footpaths all wet with dew, and so regain my ship.

Alas! in the days gone by, it was the cry of the muezzin which used to awaken me in the dark winter mornings in faraway, night-shrouded Stamboul.

CHAPTER XXVIII

A DOLL'S CORRESPONDENCE

Chrysantheme has brought but few things with her, knowing that our domestic life would probably be brief.

She has placed her gowns and her fine sashes in little closed recesses, hidden in one of the walls of our apartment (the north wall, the only one of the four which can not be taken to pieces). The doors of these niches are white paper panels; the standing shelves and inside partitions, consisting of light woodwork, are put together almost too finically and too ingeniously, giving rise to suspicions of secret drawers and conjuring tricks. We put there only things without any value, having a vague feeling that the cupboards themselves might spirit them away.

The box in which Chrysantheme stores away her gewgaws and letters, is one of the things that amuse me most; it is of English make, tin, and bears on its cover the colored representation of some manufactory in the neighborhood of London. Of course, it is as an exotic work of art, as a precious knickknack, that Chrysantheme prefers it to any of her other boxes in lacquer or inlaid work. It contains all that a mousme requires for her correspondence: Indian ink, a paintbrush, very thin, gray-tinted paper, cut up in long narrow strips, and odd-shaped envelopes, into which these strips are slipped (having been folded up in about thirty folds); the envelopes are ornamented with pictures of landscapes, fishes, crabs, or birds.

On some old letters addressed to her, I can make out the two characters that represent her name: Kikousan ("Chrysantheme, Madame"). And when I question her, she replies in Japanese, with an air of importance:

"My dear, they are letters from my woman friends."

Oh, those friends of Chrysantheme, what funny little faces they have! That same box contains their portraits, their photographs stuck on visiting cards, which are printed on the back with the name of Uyeno, the fashionable photographer in Nagasaki—the little creatures fit only to figure daintily on painted fans, who have striven to assume a dignified attitude when once their necks have been placed in the head-rest, and they have been told: "Now, don't move."

It would really amuse me to read the letters of my mousme's friends—and above all her replies !

CHAPTER XXIX

SUDDEN SHOWERS

August 10th.

It rained this evening heavily, and the night was close and dark. About ten o'clock, on our return from one of the fashionable tea-houses we frequent, we arrived—Yves, Chrysantheme and I—at the familiar angle of the principal street, the turn where we must take leave of the lights and noises of the town, to climb up the dark steps and steep paths that lead to our dwelling at Diou-djen-dji.

But before beginning our ascent, we must first buy lanterns from an old tradeswoman called Madame Tres-Propre, whose regular customers we are. It is amazing what a quantity of these paper lanterns we consume. They are invariably decorated in the same way, with painted nightmoths or bats; fastened to the ceiling at the farther end of the shop, they hang in enormous clusters, and the old woman, seeing us arrive, gets upon a table to take them down. Gray or red are our usual choice; Madame Tres- Propre knows our preferences and leaves the green or blue lanterns aside. But it is always hard work to unhook one, on account of the little short sticks by which they are held, and the strings with which they are tied getting entangled together. In an exaggerated pantomime, Madame Tres- Propre expresses her despair at wasting so much of our valuable time: oh! if it only depended on her personal efforts! but ah! the natural perversity of inanimate things which have no consideration for human dignity! With monkeyish antics, she even deems it her duty to threaten the lanterns and shake her fist at these inextricably tangled strings which have the presumption to delay us.

It is all very well, but we know this manoeuvre by heart; and if the old lady loses patience, so do we.

Chrysantheme, who is half asleep, is seized with a fit of kitten-like yawning which she does not even trouble to hide behind her hand, and which appears to be endless. She pulls a very long face at the thought of the steep hill we must struggle up tonight through the pelting rain.

I have the same feeling, and am thoroughly annoyed. To what purpose do I clamber up every evening to that suburb, when it offers me no attractions whatever?

The rain increases; what are we to do? Outside, djins pass rapidly, calling out: "Take care!" splashing the foot-passengers and casting through the shower streams of light from their many-colored lanterns. Mousmes and elderly ladies pass, tucked up, muddy, laughing nevertheless under their paper umbrellas, exchanging greetings, clacking their wooden pattens on the stone pavement. The whole street is filled with the noise of the pattering feet and pattering rain.

As good luck will have it, at the same moment passes Number 415, our poor relative, who, seeing our distress, stops and promises to help us out of our difficulty; as soon as he has deposited on the quay an Englishman he is conveying, he will come to our aid and bring all that is necessary to relieve us from our lamentable situation.

At last our lantern is unhooked, lighted, and paid for. There is another shop opposite, where we stop every evening; it is that of Madame L'Heure[1], the woman who sells waffles; we always buy a provision from her, to refresh us on the way. A very lively young woman is this pastry-cook, and most eager to make herself agreeable; she looks quite like a screen picture behind her piled-up cakes, ornamented with little posies. We will take shelter under her roof while we wait; and, to avoid the drops that

---

[1] 'Toki-San' in japanese, 'toki' means the time, the moment *(Editor footnote)*.

fall heavily from the waterspouts, wedge ourselves tightly against her display of white and pink sweetmeats, so artistically spread out on fresh and delicate branches of cypress.

Poor Number 415, what a providence he is to us! Already he reappears, most excellent cousin! ever smiling, ever running, while the water streams down his handsome bare legs; he brings us two umbrellas, borrowed from a China merchant, who is also a distant relative of ours. Like me, Yves has till now never consented to use such a thing, but he now accepts one because it is droll: of paper, of course, with innumerable folds waxed and gummed, and the inevitable flight of storks forming a wreath around it.

Chrysantheme, yawning more and more in her kitten-like fashion, becomes coaxing in order to be helped along, and tries to take my arm.

"I beg you, mousme, this evening to take the arm of Yves-San; I am sure that will suit us all three."

And there they go, she, tiny figure, hanging on to the big fellow, and so they climb up. I lead the way, carrying the lantern that lights our steps, whose flame I protect as well as I can under my fantastic umbrella. On each side of the road is heard the roaring torrent of stormy waters rolling down from the mountain-side. To-night the way seems long, difficult, and slippery; a succession of interminable flights of steps, gardens, and houses piled up one above another; waste lands, and trees which in the darkness shake their dripping foliage on our heads.

One would say that Nagasaki is ascending at the same time as ourselves; but yonder, and very far away, is a vapory mist which seems luminous against the blackness of the sky, and from the town rises a confused murmur of voices and laughter, and a rumbling of gongs.

The summer rain has not yet refreshed the atmosphere. On account of the stormy heat, the little suburban houses have been left open like sheds, and we can see all that is going on. Lamps burn perpetually before the altars dedicated to Buddha and to the souls of the ancestors; but all good Nipponese have already lain down to rest. Under the traditional tents of bluish-green gauze, we can see whole families stretched out in rows; they are either sleeping, or hunting the mosquitoes, or fanning themselves. Nipponese men and women, Nipponese babies too, lying side by side with their parents; each one, young or old, in his little dark-blue cotton nightdress, and with his little wooden block on which to rest the nape of his neck.

A few houses are open, where amusements are still going on; here and there, from the sombre gardens, the sound of a guitar reaches our ears, playing some dance which gives in its weird rhythm a strange impression of sadness.

Here is the well, surrounded by bamboos, where we are wont to make a nocturnal halt for Chrysantheme to take breath. Yves begs me to throw forward the red gleam of my lantern, in order to recognize the place, for it marks our halfway resting-place.

And at last, at last, here is our house! The door is closed, all is silent and dark. Our panels have been carefully shut by M. Sucre and Madame Prune; the rain streams down the wood of our old black walls.

In such weather it is impossible to allow Yves to return down hill, and wander along the shore in quest of a sampan. No, he shall not return on board to-night; we will put him up in our house. His little room has indeed been already provided for in the conditions of our lease, and notwithstanding his discreet refusal, we immediately set to work to make it. Let us go in, take off our boots, shake ourselves like so many cats that have been out in a shower, and step up to our apartment.

In front of Buddha, the little lamps are burning; in the middle of the room, the night-blue gauze is stretched.

On entering, the first impression is favorable; our dwelling is pretty this evening; the late hour and deep silence give it an air of mystery. And then, in such weather, it is always pleasant to get home.

Come, let us at once prepare Yves's room. Chrysantheme, quite elated at the prospect of having her big friend near her, sets to work with a good will; moreover, the task is easy; we have only to slip three or four paper panels in their grooves, to make at once a separate room or compartment in the great box we live in. I had thought that these panels were entirely white; but no! on each is a group of two storks painted in gray tints in those inevitable attitudes consecrated by Japanese art: one bearing aloft its proud head and haughtily raising its leg, the other scratching itself. Oh, these storks! how tired one gets of them, at the end of a month spent in Japan!

Yves is now in bed and sleeping under our roof.

Sleep has come to him sooner than to me to-night; for somehow I fancy I had seen long glances exchanged between him and Chrysantheme.

I have left this little creature in his hands like a toy, and I begin to fear lest I should have caused some perturbation in his mind. I do not trouble my head about this little Japanese girl. But Yves—it would be decidedly wrong on his part, and would greatly diminish my faith in him.

We hear the rain falling on our old roof; the cicalas are mute; odors of wet earth reach us from the gardens and the mountain. I feel terribly dreary in this room to-night; the noise of the little pipe irritates me more than usual, and as Chrysantheme crouches in front of her smoking- box, I suddenly discover in her an air of low breeding, in the very worst sense of the word.

I should hate her, my mousme, if she were to entice Yves into committing a fault—a fault which I should perhaps never be able to forgive.

CHAPTER XXX

A LITTLE DOMESTIC DIFFICULTY

August 12th.

The Y* and Sikou-San couple were divorced yesterday. The Charles N* and Campanule household is getting on very badly. They have had some trouble with those prying, grinding, insupportable little men, dressed up in gray suits, who are called police agents, and who, by threatening their landlord, have had them turned out of their house (under the obsequious amiability of this people lurks a secret hatred toward Europeans)—they are therefore obliged to accept their mother-in-law's hospitality, a very disagreeable situation. And then Charles N* fancies his mousme is faithless. It is hardly possible, however, for us to deceive ourselves: these would-be maidens, to whom M. Kangourou has introduced us, have already had in their lives one adventure, at least, and perhaps more; it is therefore only natural that we should have our suspicions.

The Z* and Touki-San couple jog on, quarrelling all the time.

My household maintains a more dignified air, though it is none the less dreary. I had indeed thought of a divorce, but have really no good reason for offering Chrysantheme such a gratuitous affront; moreover, there is another more imperative reason why I should remain quiet: I, too, have had difficulties with the civilian authorities.

The day before yesterday, M. Sucre, quite upset, Madame Prune, almost swooning, and Mademoiselle Oyouki, bathed in tears, stormed my rooms. The Nipponese police agents had called and threatened them with the law for letting rooms outside of the European concession to a Frenchman morganatically[1] married to a Japanese; and the terror of being prosecuted brought them to me, with a thousand apologies, but with the humble request that I should leave.

The next day I therefore went off, accompanied by "the wonderfully tall friend"—who expresses himself in Japanese better than I to the registry office, with the full intention of making a terrible row.

In the language of this exquisitely polite people, terms of abuse are totally wanting; when very angry, one is obliged to be satisfied with using the 'thou', a mark of inferiority, and the familiar conjugation, habitually used toward those of low birth. Sitting upon the table used for weddings, among the flurried little policemen, I opened the conversation in the following terms:

"In order that thou shouldst leave me in peace in the suburb I am inhabiting, what bribe must I offer thee, oh, little beings more contemptible than any mere street porter?"

Great and general dismay, silent consternation, and low bows greet my words.

They at last reply that my honorable person shall not be molested, indeed, they ask for nothing better. Only, in order to subscribe to the laws of the country, I ought to have come here and given my name and that of the young person that—with whom—

---

[1] In the context of royalty, a morganatic marriage is a marriage between people of unequal social rank *(Editor footnote)*.

"Oh! that is going too far! I came here for that purpose, contemptible creatures, not three weeks ago!"

Then, taking up myself the civil register, and turning over the pages rapidly, I found my signature and beside it the little hieroglyphics drawn by Chrysantheme:

"There, idiots, look at that!"

Arrival of a very high functionary—a ridiculous little old fellow in a black coat, who from his office had been listening to the row:

"What is the matter? What is it? What is this annoyance put upon the French officers?"

I state my case politely to this personage, who can not make apologies and promises enough. The little agents prostrate themselves on all fours, sink into the earth; and we leave them, cold and dignified, without returning their bows.

M. Sucre and Madame Prune may now make their minds easy; they will not be disturbed again.

CHAPTER XXXI

BUTTERFLIES AND BEETLES

August 23d.

The prolonged sojourn of the Triomphante in the dock, and the distance of our dwelling from the town, have been my excuse these last two or three days for not going up to Diou-djen-dji to see Chrysantheme.

It is dreary work in these docks. At early dawn a legion of little Japanese workmen invade us, bringing their dinners in baskets and gourds like the workingmen in our arsenals, but with a poor, shabby appearance, and a ferreting, hurried manner which reminds one of rats.

Silently they slip under the keel, at the bottom of the hold, in all the holes, sawing, nailing, repairing.

The heat is intense in this spot, overshadowed by the rocks and tangled masses of foliage.

At two o'clock, in the broad sunlight, we have a new and far prettier invasion: that of the beetles and butterflies.

There are butterflies as wonderful as those on the fans. Some, all black, giddily dash up against us, so light and airy that they seem merely a pair of quivering wings fastened together without any body.

Yves, astonished, gazes at them, saying, in his boyish manner: "Oh, I saw such a big one just now, such a big one, it quite frightened me; I thought it was a bat attacking me."

A steersman who has captured a very curious specimen carries it off carefully to press between the leaves of his signal-book, like a flower. Another sailor, passing by, taking his small roast to the oven in a mess-bowl, looks at him quizzically and says:

"You had much better give it to me. I'd cook it!"

CHAPTER XXXII

STRANGE YEARNINGS

August 24th.

Nearly five days have passed since I abandoned my little house and Chrysantheme.

Since yesterday we have had a tremendous storm of rain and wind (a typhoon that has passed or is passing over us). We beat to quarters in the middle of the night to lower the topmasts, strike the lower yards, and take every precaution against bad weather. The butterflies no longer hover around us; everything tosses and writhes overhead: on the steep slopes of the mountain the trees shiver, the long grasses bend low as if in pain; terrible gusts rack them with a hissing sound; branches, bamboo leaves, and earth fall like rain upon us.

In this land of pretty little trifles, this violent tempest is out of harmony; it seems as if its efforts were exaggerated and its music too loud.

Toward evening the dark clouds roll by so rapidly that the showers are of short duration and soon pass over. Then I attempt a walk on the mountain above us, in the wet verdure: little pathways lead up it, between thickets of camellias and bamboo.

Waiting till a shower is over, I take refuge in the courtyard of an old temple halfway up the hill, buried in a wood of century plants with gigantic branches; it is reached by granite steps, through strange gateways, as deeply furrowed as the old Celtic dolmens. The trees have also invaded this yard; the daylight is overcast with a greenish tint, and the drenching torrent of rain is full of torn-up leaves and moss. Old granite monsters, of unknown shapes, are seated in the corners, and grimace with smiling ferocity: their faces are full of indefinable mystery that makes me shudder amid the moaning music of the wind, in the gloomy shadows of the clouds and branches.

They could not have resembled the Japanese of our day, the men who had thus conceived these ancient temples, who built them everywhere, and filled the country with them, even in its most solitary nooks.

An hour later, in the twilight of that stormy day, on the same mountain, I encountered a clump of trees somewhat similar to oaks in appearance; they, too, have been twisted by the tempest, and the tufts of undulating grass at their feet are laid low, tossed about in every direction. There was suddenly brought back to my mind my first impression of a strong wind in the woods of Limoise, in the province of Saintonge, twenty-eight years ago, in a month of March of my childhood.

That, the first wind-storm my eyes ever beheld sweeping over the landscape, blew in just the opposite quarter of the world (and many years have rapidly passed over that memory), the spot where the best part of my life has been spent.

I refer too often, I fancy, to my childhood; I am foolishly fond of it. But it seems to me that then only did I truly experience sensations or impressions; the smallest trifles I saw or heard then were full of deep and hidden meaning, recalling past images out of oblivion, and reawakening memories of prior existences; or else they were presentiments of existences to come, future incarnations in the land of dreams, expectations of wondrous marvels that life and the world held in store for me-for a later period, no doubt, when I should be grown up. Well, I have grown up, and have found nothing that answered to my indefinable expectations; on the contrary, all has narrowed and darkened around me, my vague recollections of the past have become blurred, the horizons before me have slowly closed in and become full of gray darkness. Soon will my time come to return to eternal rest, and I shall leave this world without ever having understood the mysterious cause of these mirages of my childhood; I shall bear away with me a lingering regret for I know not what lost home that I have failed to find, of the unknown beings ardently longed for, whom, alas, I never have embraced.

CHAPTER XXXIII

A GENEROUS HUSBAND

Displaying many affectations, M. Sucre dips the tip of his delicate paint-brush in India-ink and traces a pair of charming storks on a pretty sheet of rice-paper, offering them to me in the most courteous manner, as a souvenir of himself. I have put them in my cabin on board, and when I look at them, I fancy I can see M. Sucre tracing them with an airy touch and with elegant facility.

The saucer in which he mixes his ink is in itself a little gem. It is chiselled out of a piece of jade, and represents a tiny lake with a carved border imitating rockwork. On this border is a little mamma toad, also in jade, advancing as if to bathe in the little lake in which M. Sucre carefully keeps a few drops of very dark liquid. The mamma toad has four little baby toads, in jade, one perched on her head, the other three playing about under her.

M. Sucre has painted many a stork in the course of his lifetime, and he really excels in reproducing groups and duets, if one may so express it, of this bird. Few Japanese possess the art of interpreting this subject in a manner at once so rapid and so tasteful; first he draws the two beaks, then the four claws, then the backs, the feathers, dash, dash, dash—with a dozen strokes of his clever brush, held in his daintily posed hand, it is done, and always perfectly well done!

M. Kangourou relates, without seeing anything wrong in it whatever, that formerly this talent was of great service to M. Sucre. It appears that Madame Prune—how shall I say such a thing, and, who could guess it now, on beholding so devout and sedate an old lady, with eyebrows so scrupulously shaven?—however, it appears that Madame Prune used to receive a great many visits from gentlemen—gentlemen who always came alone—which led to some gossip. Therefore, when Madame Prune was engaged with one visitor, if a new arrival made his appearance, the ingenious husband, to induce him to wait patiently, and to wile away the time in the anteroom, immediately offered to paint him some storks in a variety of attitudes.

And this is why, in Nagasaki, all the Japanese gentlemen of a certain age have in their collections two or three of these little pictures, for which they are indebted to the delicate and original talent of M. Sucre!

CHAPTER XXXIV

THE FEAST OF THE TEMPLE

Sunday, August 25th.

About six o'clock, while I was on duty, the 'Triomphante' abandoned her prison walls between the mountains and came out of dock. After much manoeuvring we took up our old moorings in the harbor, at the foot of the Diou-djen-dji hills. The weather was again calm and cloudless, the sky presenting a peculiar clarity, as if it had been swept by a cyclone, an exceeding transparency bringing out the minutest details in the distance till then unseen; as if the terrible blast had blown away every vestige of the floating mists and left behind it nothing but void and boundless space. The coloring of woods and mountains stood out again in the resplendent verdancy of spring after the torrents of rain, like the wet colors of some freshly washed painting. The sampans and junks, which for the last three days had been lying under shelter, had now put out to sea, and the bay was covered with their white sails, which looked like a flight of enormous seabirds.

At eight o'clock, at nightfall, our manoeuvres having ended, I embarked with Yves on board a sampan; this time it is he who is carrying me off and taking me back to my home.

On land, a delicious perfume of new-mown hay greets us, and the road across the mountains is bathed in glorious moonlight. We go straight up to Diou-djen-dji to join Chrysantheme; I feel almost remorseful, although I hardly show it, for my neglect of her.

Looking up, I recognize from afar my little house, perched on high. It is wide open and lighted; I even hear the sound of a guitar. Then I perceive the gilt head of my Buddha between the little bright flames of its two hanging night-lamps. Now Chrysantheme appears on the veranda, looking out as if she expected us; and with her wonderful bows of hair and long, falling sleeves, her silhouette is thoroughly Nipponese.

As I enter, she comes forward to kiss me, in a graceful, though rather hesitating manner, while Oyouki, more demonstrative, throws her arms around me.

Not without a certain pleasure do I see once more this Japanese home, which I wonder to find still mine when I had almost forgotten its existence. Chrysantheme has put fresh flowers in our vases, spread out her hair, donned her best clothes, and lighted our lamps to honor my return. From the balcony she had watched the 'Triomphante' leave the dock, and, in the expectation of our prompt return, she had made her preparations; then, to wile away the time, she was studying a duet on the guitar with Oyouki. Not a question did she ask, nor a reproach did she make. Quite the contrary.

"We understood," she said, "how impossible it was, in such dreadful weather, to undertake so lengthy a crossing in a sampan."

She smiled like a pleased child, and I should be fastidious indeed if I did not admit that to-night she is charming.

I announce my intention of taking a long stroll through Nagasaki; we will take Oyouki-San and two little cousins who happen to be here, as well as some other neighbors, if they wish it; we will buy the most amusing toys, eat all sorts of cakes, and entertain ourselves to our hearts' content.

"How lucky we are to be here, just at the right moment," they exclaim, jumping with joy. "How fortunate we are! This very evening there is to be a pilgrimage to the great temple of the jumping Tortoise! "The whole town will be there; all our married friends have already started, the whole set, X*, Y*, Z*, Toki-San, Campanule, and Jonquille, with "the friend of amazing height." And these two, poor Chrysantheme and poor Oyouki, would have been obliged to stay at home with heavy hearts, had we not arrived, because Madame Prune had been seized with faintness and hysterics after her dinner.

Quickly the mousmes must deck themselves out. Chrysantheme is ready; Oyouki hurries, changes her dress, and, putting on a mouse-colored gray robe, begs me to arrange the bows of her fine sash-black satin lined with yellow-sticking at the same time in her hair a silver topknot. We light our lanterns, swinging at the end of little sticks; M. Sucre, overwhelming us with thanks for his daughter, accompanies us on all fours to the door, and we go off gayly through the clear and balmy night.

Below, we find the town in all the animation of a great holiday. The streets are thronged; the crowd passes by—a laughing, capricious, slow, unequal tide, flowing onward, however, steadily in the same direction, toward the same goal. From it rises a penetrating but light murmur, in which dominate the sounds of laughter, and the low-toned interchange of polite speeches. Then follow lanterns upon lanterns. Never in my life have I seen so many, so variegated, so complicated, and so extraordinary.

We follow, drifting with the surging crowd, borne along by it. There are groups of women of every age, decked out in their smartest clothes, crowds of mousmes with aigrettes of flowers in their hair, or little silver topknots like Oyouki—pretty little physiognomies, little, narrow eyes peeping between their slits like those of new-born kittens, fat, pale, little cheeks, round, puffed-out, half-opened lips. They are pretty, nevertheless, these little Nipponese, in their smiles and childishness.

The men, on the other hand, wear many a pot-hat, pompously added to the long national robe, and giving thereby a finishing touch to their cheerful ugliness, resembling nothing so much as dancing monkeys. They carry boughs in their hands, whole shrubs even, amid the foliage of which dangle all sorts of curious lanterns in the shapes of imps and birds.

As we advance in the direction of the temple, the streets become more noisy and crowded. All along the houses are endless stalls raised on trestles, displaying sweetmeats of every color, toys, branches of flowers, nosegays and masks. There are masks everywhere, boxes full of them, carts full of them; the most popular being the one that represents the livid and cunning muzzle, contracted as by a deathlike grimace, the long straight ears and sharp-pointed teeth of the white fox, sacred to the God of Rice. There are also others symbolic of gods or monsters, livid, grimacing, convulsed, with wigs and beards of natural hair. All manner of folk, even children, purchase these horrors, and fasten them over their faces. Every sort of instrument is for sale, among them many of those crystal trumpets which sound so strangely—this evening they are enormous, six feet long at least—and the noise they make is unlike anything ever heard before: one would say gigantic turkeys were gobbling amid the crowd, striving to inspire fear.

In the religious amusements of this people it is not possible for us to penetrate the mysteriously hidden meaning of things; we can not divine the boundary at which jesting stops and mystic fear steps in. These customs, these symbols, these masks, all that tradition and atavism have jumbled together in the Japanese brain, proceed from sources utterly dark and unknown to us; even the oldest records fail to explain them to us in anything but a superficial and cursory manner, simply because we have absolutely nothing in common with this people. We pass through the midst of their mirth and their laughter without understanding the wherefore, so totally do they differ from our own.

Chrysantheme with Yves, Oyouki with me, Fraise and Zinnia, our cousins, walking before us under our watchful eyes, move slowly through the crowd, holding hands lest we should lose one another.

Along the streets leading to the temple, the wealthy inhabitants have decorated the fronts of their houses with vases and nosegays. The peculiar shed-like buildings common in this country, with their open platform frontage, are particularly well suited for the display of choice objects; all the houses have been thrown open, and the interiors are hung with draperies that hide the back of the apartments. In front of these hangings, and standing slightly back from the movement of the passing crowd, the various exhibited articles are placed methodically in a row, under the full glare of hanging lamps. Hardly any flowers compose the nosegays, nothing but foliage— some rare and priceless, others chosen, as if purposely, from the commonest plants, arranged, however, with such taste as to make them appear new and choice; ordinary lettuce-leaves, tall cabbage-stalks are placed with exquisite artificial taste in vessels of marvellous workmanship. All the vases are of bronze, but the designs are varied according to each changing fancy: some complicated and twisted, others, and by far the larger number, graceful and simple, but of a simplicity so studied and exquisite that to our eyes they seem the revelation of an unknown art, the subversion of all acquired notions of form.

On turning a corner of a street, by good luck we meet our married comrades of the Triomphante and Jonquille, Toukisan and Campanule! Bows and curtseys are exchanged by the mousmes, reciprocal manifestations of joy at meeting; then, forming a compact band, we are carried off by the ever-increasing crowd and continue our progress in the direction of the temple.

The streets gradually ascend (the temples are always built on a height); and by degrees, as we mount, there is added to the brilliant fairyland of lanterns and costumes yet another, ethereally blue in the haze of distance; all Nagasaki, its pagodas, its mountains, its still waters full of the rays of moonlight, seem to rise with us into the air. Slowly, step by step, one may say it springs up around, enveloping in one great shimmering veil all the foreground, with its dazzling red lights and many-colored streamers.

No doubt we are drawing near, for here are steps, porticoes and monsters hewn out of enormous blocks of granite. We now have to climb a series of steps, almost carried by the surging crowd ascending with us.

We have arrived at the temple courtyard.

This is the last and most astonishing scene in the evening's fairy-tale —a luminous and weird scene, with fantastic distances lighted up by the moon, with the gigantic trees, the sacred cryptomerias, elevating their sombre boughs into a vast dome.

Here we are all seated with our mousmés, beneath the light awning, wreathed in flowers, of one of the many little teahouses improvised in this courtyard. We are on a terrace at the top of the great steps, up which the crowd continues to flock, and at the foot of a portico which stands erect with the rigid massiveness of a colossus against the dark night sky; at the foot also of a monster, who stares down upon us, with his big stony eyes, his cruel grimace and smile.

This portico and the monster are the two great overwhelming masses in the foreground of the incredible scene before us; they stand out with dazzling boldness against the vague and ashy blue of the distant sphere beyond; behind them, Nagasaki is spread out in a bird's-eye view, faintly outlined in the transparent darkness with myriads of little colored lights, and the extravagantly dented profile of the mountains is delineated on the starlit sky, blue upon blue, transparency upon transparency. A corner of the harbor also is visible, far up, undefined, like a lake lost in clouds the water, faintly illumined by a ray of moonlight, making it shine like a sheet of silver.

Around us the long crystal trumpets keep up their gobble. Groups of polite and frivolous persons pass and repass like fantastic shadows: childish bands of small-eyed mousmés with smile so candidly meaningless and coiffures shining through their bright silver flowers; ugly men waving at the end of long branches their eternal lanterns shaped like birds, gods, or insects.

Behind us, in the illuminated and wide-open temple, the bonzes sit, immovable embodiments of doctrine, in the glittering sanctuary inhabited by divinities, chimeras, and symbols. The crowd, monotonously droning its mingled prayers and laughter, presses around them, sowing its alms broadcast; with a continuous jingle, the money rolls on the ground into the precincts reserved to the priests, where the white mats entirely f disappear under the mass of many-sized coins accumulated there as if after a deluge of silver and bronze.

We, however, feel thoroughly at sea in the midst of this festivity; we look on, we laugh like the rest, we make foolish and senseless remarks in a language insufficiently learned, which this evening, I know not why, we can hardly understand. Notwithstanding the night breeze, we find it very hot under our awning, and we absorb quantities of odd-looking water-ices, served in cups, which taste like scented frost, or rather like flowers steeped in snow. Our mousmes order for themselves great bowls of candied beans mixed with hail—real hailstones, such as we might pick up after a hailstorm in March.

Glou! glou! glou! the crystal trumpets slowly repeat their notes, the powerful sonority of which has a labored and smothered sound, as if they came from under water; they mingle with the jingling of rattles and the noise of castanets. We have also the impression of being carried away in the irresistible swing of this incomprehensible gayety, composed, in proportions we can hardly measure, of elements mystic, puerile, and even ghastly. A sort of religious terror is diffused by the hidden idols divined in the temple behind us; by the mumbled prayers, confusedly heard; above all, by the horrible heads in lacquered wood, representing foxes, which, as they pass, hide human faces—hideous livid masks.

In the gardens and outbuildings of the temple the most inconceivable mountebanks have taken up their quarters, their black streamers, painted with white letters, looking like funeral trappings as they float in the wind from the tops of their tall flagstaffs. Thither we turn our steps, as soon as our mousmes have ended their orisons and bestowed their alms.

In one of the booths a man, stretched on a table, flat on his back, is alone on the stage; puppets of almost human size, with horribly grinning masks, spring out of his body; they speak, gesticulate, then fall back like empty rags; with a sudden spring they start up again, change their costumes, change their faces, tearing about in one continual frenzy. Suddenly three, even four, appear at the same time; they are nothing more than the four limbs of the outstretched man, whose legs and arms, raised on high, are each dressed up and capped with a wig under which peers a mask; between these phantoms tremendous fighting and battling take place, and many a sword-thrust is exchanged. The most fearful of all is a certain puppet representing an old hag; every time she appears, with her weird head and ghastly grin, the lights burn low, the music of the accompanying orchestra moans forth a sinister strain given by the flutes, mingled with a rattling tremolo which sounds like the clatter of bones. This creature evidently plays an ugly part in the piece—that of a horrible old ghoul, spiteful and famished. Still more appalling than her person is her shadow, which, projected upon a white screen, is abnormally and vividly distinct; by means of some unknown process this shadow, which nevertheless follows all her movements, assumes the aspect of a wolf. At a given moment the hag turns round and presents the profile of her distorted snub nose as she accepts the bowl of rice which is offered to her; on the screen at the very same instant appears the elongated outline of the wolf, with its pointed ears, its muzzle and chops, its great teeth and hanging tongue. The orchestra grinds, wails, quivers; then suddenly bursts out into funereal shrieks, like a concert of owls; the hag is now eating, and her wolfish shadow is eating also, greedily moving its jaws and nibbling at another shadow easy to recognize—the arm of a little child.

We now go on to see the great salamander of Japan, an animal rare in this country, and quite unknown elsewhere, a great, cold mass, sluggish and benumbed, looking like some antediluvian experiment, forgotten in the inner seas of this archipelago.

Next comes the trained elephant, the terror of our mousmes, the equilibrists, the menagerie.

It is one o'clock in the morning before we are back at Diou-djen-dji.

We first get Yves to bed in the little paper room he has already once occupied. Then we go to bed ourselves, after the inevitable preparations, the smoking of the little pipe, and the tap! tap! tap! tap! on the edge of the box.

Suddenly Yves begins to move restlessly in his sleep, to toss about, giving great kicks on the wall, and making a frightful noise.

What can be the matter? I imagine at once that he must be dreaming of the old hag and her wolfish shadow. Chrysantheme raises herself on her elbow and listens, with astonishment depicted on her face.

Ah, happy thought! she has guessed what is tormenting him:

"Ka!" ("mosquitoes") she says.

And, to impress the more forcibly her meaning on my mind, she pinches my arm so hard with her little pointed nails, at the same time imitating, with such an amusing play of her features, the grimace of a person who is stung, that I exclaim:

"Oh! stop, Chrysantheme, this pantomime is too expressive, and indeed useless! I know the word 'Ka', and had quite understood, I assure you."

It is done so drolly and so quickly, with such a pretty pout, that in truth I can not think of being angry, although I shall certainly have tomorrow a blue mark on my arm; about that there is no doubt.

"Come, we must get up and go to Yves's rescue; he must not be allowed to go on thumping in that manner. Let us take a lantern, and see what has happened."

It was indeed the mosquitoes. They are hovering in a thick cloud about him; those of the house and those of the garden all seem collected together, swarming and buzzing. Chrysantheme indignantly burns several at the flame of her lantern, and shows me others (Hou!) covering the white paper walls.

He, tired out with his day's amusement, sleeps on; but his slumbers are restless, as may be easily imagined. Chrysantheme gives him a shake, wishing him to get up and share our blue mosquito-net.

After a little pressing he does as he is bid and follows us, looking like an overgrown boy only half awake. I make no objection to this singular hospitality; after all, it looks so little like a bed, the matting we are to share, and we sleep in our clothes, as we always do, according to the Nipponese fashion. After all, on a journey in a railway, do not the most estimable ladies stretch themselves without demur by the side of gentlemen unknown to them?

I have, however, placed Chrysantheme's little wooden block in the centre of the gauze tent, between our two pillows.

Without saying a word, in a dignified manner, as if she were rectifying an error of etiquette that I had inadvertently committed, Chrysantheme takes up her piece of wood, putting in its place my snake-skin drum; I shall therefore be in the middle between the two. It is really more correct, decidedly more proper; Chrysantheme is evidently a very decorous young person.

Returning on board next morning, in the clear morning sun, we walk through pathways full of dew, accompanied by a band of funny little mousmes of six or eight years of age, who are going to school.

Needless to say, the cicalas around us keep up their perpetual sonorous chirping. The mountain smells delicious. The atmosphere, the dawning day, the infantine grace of these little girls in their long frocks and shiny coiffures-all is redundant with freshness and youth. The flowers and grasses on which we tread sparkle with dewdrops, exhaling a perfume of freshness. What undying beauty there is, even in Japan, in the fresh morning hours in the country, and the dawning hours of life!

Besides, I am quite ready to admit the attractiveness of the little Japanese children; some of them are most fascinating. But how is it that their charm vanishes so rapidly and is so quickly replaced by the elderly grimace, the smiling ugliness, the monkeyish face ?

CHAPTER XXXV

THROUGH A MICROSCOPE

The small garden of my mother-in-law, Madame Renoncule, is, without exception, one of the most melancholy spots I have seen in all my travels through the world.

Oh, the slow, enervating, dull hours spent in idle and diffuse conversation on the dimly lighted veranda! Oh, the detestable peppered jam in the tiny pots! In the middle of the town, enclosed by four walls, is this park of five yards square, with little lakes, little mountains, and little rocks, where all wears an antiquated appearance, and everything is covered with a greenish mold from want of sunlight.

Nevertheless, a true feeling for nature has inspired this tiny representation of a wild spot. The rocks are well placed, the dwarf cedars, no taller than cabbages, stretch their gnarled boughs over the valleys in the attitude of giants wearied by the weight of centuries; and their look of full-grown trees perplexes one and falsifies the perspective. When from the dark recesses of the apartment one perceives at a certain distance this diminutive landscape dimly lighted, the wonder is whether it is all artificial, or whether one is not one's self the victim of some morbid illusion; and whether it is not indeed a real country view seen through a distorted vision out of focus, or through the wrong end of a telescope.

To any one familiar with Japanese life, my mother-in-law's house in itself reveals a refined nature—complete bareness, two or three screens placed here and there, a teapot, a vase full of lotus-flowers, and nothing more. Woodwork devoid of paint or varnish, but carved in most elaborate and capricious openwork, the whiteness of the pinewood being preserved by constant scrubbing with soap and water. The posts and beams of the framework are varied by the most fanciful taste: some are cut in precise geometrical forms; others are artificially twisted, imitating trunks of old trees covered with tropical creepers. Everywhere are little hiding-places, little nooks, little closets concealed in the most ingenious and unexpected manner under the immaculate uniformity of the white paper panels.

I can not help smiling when I think of some of the so-called "Japanese" drawing-rooms of our Parisian fine ladies, overcrowded with knickknacks and curios and hung with coarse gold embroideries on exported satins. I would advise those persons to come and look at the houses of people of taste out here; to visit the white solitudes of the palaces at Yeddo[1]. In France we have works of art in order to enjoy them; here they possess them merely to ticket them and lock them up carefully in

---

[1] Yedo or Edo until 1868, the end of shogunate *(Editor footnote)*.

a kind of mysterious underground room called a 'godoun', shut in by iron gratings. On rare occasions, only to honor some visitor of distinction, do they open this impenetrable depositary. The true Japanese manner of understanding luxury consists in a scrupulous and indeed almost excessive cleanliness, white mats and white woodwork; an appearance of extreme simplicity, and an incredible nicety in the most infinitesimal details.

My mother-in-law seems to be really a very good woman, and were it not for the insurmountable feeling of spleen the sight of her garden produces on me, I should often go to see her. She has nothing in common with the mammas of Jonquille, Campanule, or Touki she is vastly their superior; and then I can see that she has been very good-looking and fashionable. Her past life puzzles me; but, in my position as a son-in-law, good manners prevent my making further inquiries.

Some assert that she was formerly a celebrated geisha in Yeddo, who lost public favor by her folly in becoming a mother. This would account for her daughter's talent on the guitar; she had probably herself taught her the touch and style of the Conservatory.

Since the birth of Chrysantheme (her eldest child and first cause of this loss of favor), my mother-in-law, an expansive although distinguished nature, has fallen seven times into the same fatal error, and I have two little sisters-in-law: Mademoiselle La Neige,—[Oyouki-San]—and Mademoiselle La Lune,—[Tsouki-San.]—as well as five little brothers- in-law: Cerisier, Pigeon, Liseron, Or, and Bambou.

Little Bambou is four years old—a yellow baby, fat and round all over, with fine bright eyes; coaxing and jolly, sleeping whenever he is not laughing. Of all my Nipponese family, Bambou is the one I love the most.

CHAPTER XXXVI

MY NAUGHTY DOLL

Tuesday, August 27th.

During this whole day we—Yves, Chrysantheme, Oyouki and myself—have spent the time wandering through dark and dusty nooks, dragged hither and thither by four quick-footed djins, in search of antiquities in the bric- a-brac shops.

Toward sunset, Chrysantheme, who has wearied me more than ever since morning, and who doubtless has perceived it, pulls a very long face, declares herself ill, and begs leave to spend the night with her mother, Madame Renoncule.

I agree to this with the best grace in the world; let her go, tiresome little mousme! Oyouki will carry a message to her parents, who will shut up our rooms; we shall spend the evening, Yves and I, in roaming about as fancy takes us, without any mousme dragging at our heels, and shall afterward regain our own quarters on board the 'Triomphante', without having the trouble of climbing up that hill.

First of all, we make an attempt to dine together in some fashionable tea-house. Impossible! not a place is to be had; all the absurd paper rooms, all the compartments contrived by so many ingenious tricks of slipping and sliding panels, all the nooks and corners in the little gardens are filled with Japanese men and women eating impossible and incredible little dishes. Numberless young dandies are dining tete-a- tete with the ladies of their choice, and sounds of dancing-girls and music issue from the private rooms.

The fact is, to-day is the third and last day of the great pilgrimage to the temple of the jumping Tortoise, of which we saw the beginning yesterday; and all Nagasaki is at this time given over to amusement.

At the tea-house of the Indescribable Butterflies, which is also full to overflowing, but where we are well known, they have had the bright idea of throwing a temporary flooring over the little lake—the pond where the goldfish live—and our meal is served here, in the pleasant freshness of the fountain which continues its murmur under our feet.

After dinner, we follow the faithful and ascend again to the temple.

Up there we find the same elfin revelry, the same masks, the same music. We seat ourselves, as before, under a gauze tent and sip odd little drinks tasting of flowers. But this evening we are alone, and the absence of the band of mousmes, whose familiar little faces formed a bond of union between this holiday-making people and ourselves, separates and isolates us more than usual from the profusion of oddities in the midst of which we seem to be lost. Beneath us lies always the immense blue background: Nagasaki illumined by moonlight, and the expanse of silvered, glittering water, which seems like a vaporous vision suspended in mid-air. Behind us is the great open temple, where the bonzes officiate, to the accompaniment of sacred bells and wooden clappers-looking, from where we sit, more like puppets than anything else, some squatting in rows like peaceful mummies, others executing rhythmical marches before the golden background where stand the gods. We do not laugh to-night, and speak but little, more forcibly struck by the scene than we were on the first night; we only look on, trying to understand. Suddenly, Yves, turning round, says:

"Hullo! brother, there is your mousme!"

Actually, there she is, behind him; Chrysantheme, almost on all fours, hidden between the paws of a great granite beast, half tiger, half dog, against which our fragile tent is leaning.

"She pulled my trousers with her nails, for all the world like a little cat," said Yves, still full of surprise, "positively like a cat!"

She remains bent double in the most humble form of salutation; she smiles timidly, afraid of being ill received, and the head of my little brother- in-law, Bambou, appears smiling too, just above her own. She has brought this little mousko—[Mousko is the masculine of mousme, and signifies little boy. Excessive politeness makes it mousko-san (Mr. little boy).] with her, perched astride her back; he looks as absurd as ever, with his shaven head, his long frock and the great bows of his silken sash. There they stand gazing at us, anxious to know how their joke will be taken.

For my part, I have not the least idea of giving them a cold reception; on the contrary, the meeting amuses me. It even strikes me that it is rather pretty of Chrysantheme to come around in this way, and to bring Bambou-San to the festival; though it savors somewhat of her low breeding, to tell the truth, to carry him on her back, as the poorer Japanese women carry their little ones.

However, let her sit down between Yves and myself and let them bring her those iced beans she loves so much; and we will take the jolly little mousko on our knees and cram him with sugar and sweetmeats to his heart's content.

When the evening is over, and we begin to think of leaving, and of going down again, Chrysantheme replaces her little Bambou astride upon her back, and sets forth, bending forward under his weight and painfully dragging her Cinderella slippers over the granite steps and flagstones. Yes, decidedly low, this conduct! but low in the best sense of the word: nothing in it displeases me; I even consider Chrysantheme's affection for Bambou-San engaging and attractive in its simplicity.

One can not deny this merit to the Japanese—a great love for little children, and a talent for amusing them, for making them laugh, inventing comical toys for them, making the morning of their life happy; for a specialty in dressing them, arranging their heads, and giving to the whole personage the most fascinating appearance possible. It is the only thing I really like about this country: the babies and the manner in which they are understood.

On our way we meet our married friends of the Triomphante, who, much surprised at seeing me with this mousko, jokingly exclaim:

"What! a son already?"

Down in the town, we make a point of bidding goodby to Chrysantheme at the turning of the street where her mother lives. She smiles, undecided, declares herself well again, and begs to return to our house on the heights. This did not precisely enter into my plans, I confess. However, it would look very ungracious to refuse.

So be it! But we must carry the mousko home to his mamma, and then begin, by the flickering light of a new lantern bought from Madame Tres- Propre, our weary homeward ascent.

Here, however, we find ourselves in another predicament: this ridiculous little Bambou insists upon coming with us! No, he will take no denial, we must take him with us. This is out of all reason, quite impossible!

However, it will not do to make him cry, on the night of a great festival too, poor little mousko! So we must send a message to Madame Renoncule, that she may not be uneasy about him, and as there will soon not be a living creature on the footpaths of Diou-djen-dji to laugh at us, we will take it in turn, Yves and I, to carry him on our backs, all the way up that climb in the darkness.

And here am I, who did not wish to return this way tonight, dragging a mousme by the hand, and actually carrying an extra burden in the shape of a mousko on my back. What an irony of fate!

As I had expected, all our shutters and doors are closed, bolted, and barred; no one expects us, and we have to make a prodigious noise at the door. Chrysantheme sets to work and calls with all her might

"Hou   Oume-San-an-an-an!"   (In   English: "Hi! Madame Pru-u-uu-une!")

These intonations in her little voice are unknown to me; her long-drawn call in the echoing darkness of midnight has so strange an accent, something so unexpected and wild, that it impresses me with a dismal feeling of far-off exile.

At last Madame Prune appears to open the door to us, only half awake and much astonished; by way of a nightcap she wears a monstrous cotton turban, on the blue ground of which a few white storks are playfully disporting themselves. Holding in the tips of her fingers, with an affectation of graceful fright, the long stalk of her beflowered lantern, she gazes intently into our faces, one after another, to reassure herself of our identity; but the poor old lady can not get over her surprise at the sight of the mousko I am carrying.

CHAPTER XXXVII

COMPLICATIONS

At first it was only to Chrysantheme's guitar that I listened with pleasure now I am beginning to like her singing also.

She has nothing of the theatrical, or the deep, assumed voice of the virtuoso; on the contrary, her notes, always very high, are soft, thin, and plaintive.

She often teaches Oyouki some romance, slow and dreamy, which she has composed, or which comes back to her mind. Then they both astonish me, for on their well-tuned guitars they will pick out accompaniments in parts, and try again each time that the chords are not perfectly true to their ear, without ever losing themselves in the confusion of these dissonant harmonies, always weird and always melancholy.

Usually, while their music is going on, I am writing on the veranda, with the superb panorama before me. I write, seated on a mat on the floor and leaning upon a little Japanese desk, ornamented with swallows in relief; my ink is Chinese, my inkstand, just like that of my landlord, is in jade, with dear little frogs and toads carved on the rim. In short, I am writing my memoirs,—exactly as M. Sucre does downstairs! Occasionally I fancy I resemble him—a very disagreeable fancy.

My memoirs are composed of incongruous details, minute observations of colors, shapes, scents, and sounds.

It is true that a complete imbroglio, worthy of a romance, seems ever threatening to appear upon my monotonous horizon; a regular intrigue seems ever ready to explode in the midst of this little world of mousmes and grasshoppers: Chrysantheme in love with Yves; Yves with Chrysantheme; Oyouki with me; I with no one. We might even find here, ready to hand, the elements of a fratricidal drama, were we in any other country than Japan; but we are in Japan, and under the narrowing and dwarfing influence of the surroundings, which turn everything into ridicule, nothing will come of it all.

CHAPTER XXXVIII

THE HEIGHT OF SOCIABILITY!

In this fine town of Nagasaki, about five or six o'clock in the evening, one hour of the day is more comical than any other. At that moment every human being is naked: children, young people, old people, old men, old women—every one is seated in a tub of some sort, taking a bath. This ceremony takes place no matter where, without the slightest screen, in the gardens, the courtyards, in the shops, even upon the thresholds, in order to give greater facility for conversation among the neighbors from one side of the street to the other. In this situation visitors are received; and the bather, without any hesitation, leaves his tub, holding in his hand his little towel (invariably blue), to offer the caller a seat, and to exchange with him some polite remarks. Nevertheless, neither the mousmes nor the old ladies gain anything by appearing in this primeval costume. A Japanese woman, deprived of her long robe and her huge sash with its pretentious bows, is nothing but a diminutive yellow being, with crooked legs and flat, unshapely bust; she has no longer a remnant of her little artificial charms, which have completely disappeared in company with her costume.

There is yet another hour, at once joyous and melancholy, a little later, when twilight falls, when the sky seems one vast veil of yellow, against which stand the clear-cut outlines of jagged mountains and lofty, fantastic pagodas. It is the hour at which, in the labyrinth of little gray streets below, the sacred lamps begin to twinkle in the ever-open houses, in front of the ancestor's altars and the familiar Buddhas; while, outside, darkness creeps over all, and the thousand and one indentations and peaks of the old roofs are depicted, as if in black festoons, on the clear golden sky. At this moment, over merry, laughing Japan, suddenly passes a sombre shadow, strange, weird, a breath of antiquity, of savagery, of something indefinable, which casts a gloom of sadness. And then the only gayety that remains is the gayety of the young children, of little mouskos and little mousmes, who spread themselves like a wave through the streets filled with shadow, as they swarm from schools and workshops. On the dark background of all these wooden buildings, the little blue and scarlet dresses stand out in startling contrast,—drolly bedizened, drolly draped; and the fine loops of the sashes, the flowers, the silver or gold topknots stuck in these baby chignons, add to the vivid effect.

They amuse themselves, they chase one another, their great pagoda sleeves fly wide open, and these tiny little mousmes of ten, of five years old, or even younger still, have lofty head-dresses and imposing bows of hair arranged on their little heads, like grown-up women. Oh! what loves of supremely absurd dolls at this hour of twilight gambol through the streets, in their long frocks, blowing their crystal trumpets, or running with all their might to start their fanciful kites. This juvenile world of Japan—ludicrous by birth, and fated to become more so as the years roll on—starts in life with singular amusements, with strange cries and shouts; its playthings are somewhat ghastly, and would frighten the children of other countries; even the kites have great squinting eyes and vampire shapes.

And every evening, in the little dark streets, bursts forth the overflow of joyousness, fresh, childish, but withal grotesque to excess. It would be difficult to form any idea of the incredible things which, carried by the wind, float in the evening air.

CHAPTER XXXIX

A LADY OF JAPAN

My little Chrysantheme is always attired in dark colors, a sign here of aristocratic distinction. While her friends Oyouki-San, Madame Touki, and others, delight in gay-striped stuffs, and thrust gorgeous ornaments in their chignons, she always wears navy-blue or neutral gray, fastened round her waist with great black sashes brocaded in tender shades, and she puts nothing in her hair but amber-colored tortoiseshell pins. If she were of noble descent she would wear embroidered on her dress in the middle of the back a little white circle looking like a postmark with some design in the centre of it—usually the leaf of a tree; and this would be her coat-of-arms. There is really nothing wanting but this little heraldic blazon on the back to give her the appearance of a lady of the highest rank.

In Japan the smart dresses of bright colors shaded in clouds, embroidered with monsters of gold or silver, are reserved by the great ladies for home use on state occasions; or else they are used on the stage for dancers and courtesans.

Like all Japanese women, Chrysantheme carries a quantity of things in her long sleeves, in which pockets are cunningly hidden. There she keeps letters, various notes written on delicate sheets of rice-paper, prayer amulets drawn up by the bonzes; and above all a number of squares of a silky paper which she puts to the most unexpected uses—to dry a teacup, to hold the damp stalk of a flower, or to blow her quaint little nose, when the necessity presents itself. After the operation she at once crumples up the piece of paper, rolls it into a ball, and throws it out of the window with disgust.

The very smartest people in Japan blow their noses in this manner.

CHAPTER XL

OUR FRIENDS THE BONZES

September 2d.

Fate has favored us with a friendship as strange as it is rare: that of the head bonzes of the temple of the jumping Tortoise, where we witnessed last month such a surprising pilgrimage.

The approach to this place is as solitary now as it was thronged and bustling on the evenings of the festival; and in broad daylight one is surprised at the deathlike decay of the sacred surroundings which at night had seemed so full of life. Not a creature to be seen on the time- worn granite steps; not a creature beneath the vast, sumptuous porticoes; the colors, the gold-work are dim with dust. To reach the temple one must cross several deserted courtyards terraced on the mountain-side, pass through several solemn gateways, and up and up endless stairs rising far above the town and the noises of humanity into a sacred region filled with innumerable tombs. On all the pavements, in all the walls, are lichen and stonecrop; and over all the, gray tint of extreme age spreads like a fall of ashes.

In a side temple near the entrance is enthroned a colossal Buddha seated in his lotus—a gilded idol from forty-five to sixty feet high, mounted on an enormous bronze pedestal.

At length appears the last doorway with the two traditional giants, guardians of the sacred court, which stand the one on the right hand, the other on the left, shut up like wild beasts, each in an iron cage. They are in attitudes of fury, with fists upraised as if to strike, and features atrociously fierce and distorted. Their bodies are covered with bullets of crumbled paper, which have been aimed at them through the bars, and which have stuck to their monstrous limbs, producing an appearance of white leprosy: this is the manner in which the faithful strive to appease them, by conveying to them their prayers written upon delicate leaflets by the pious bonzes.

Passing between these alarming scarecrows, one reaches the innermost court. The residence of our friends is on the right, the great hall of the pagoda is before us.

In this paved court are bronze torch-holders as high as turrets. Here, too, stand, and have stood for centuries, cyca palms with fresh, green plumes, their numerous stalks curving with a heavy symmetry, like the branches of massive candelabra. The temple, which is open along its entire length, is dark and mysterious, with touches of gilding in distant corners melting away into the gloom. In the very remotest part are seated idols, and from outside one can vaguely see their clasped hands and air of rapt mysticism; in front are the altars, loaded with marvellous vases in metalwork, whence spring graceful clusters of gold and silver lotus. From the very entrance one is greeted by the sweet odor of the incense-sticks unceasingly burned by the priests before the gods.

To penetrate into the dwelling of our friends the bonzes, which is situated on the right side as you enter, is by no means an easy matter.

A monster of the fish tribe, but having claws and horns, is hung over their door by iron chains; at the least breath of wind he swings creakingly. We pass beneath him and enter the first vast and lofty hall, dimly lighted, in the corners of which gleam gilded idols, bells, and incomprehensible objects of religious use.

Quaint little creatures, choir-boys or pupils, come forward with a doubtful welcome to ask what is wanted.

"Matsou-San!! Dondta-San!!" they repeat, much astonished, when they understand to whom we wish to be conducted. Oh! no, impossible, they can not be seen; they are resting or are in contemplation. "Orimas! Orimas!" say they, clasping their hands and sketching a genuflection or two to make us understand better. ("They are at prayer! the most profound prayer!")

We insist, speak more imperatively; even slip off our shoes like people determined to take no refusal.

At last Matsou-San and Donata-San make their appearance from the tranquil depths of their bonze-house. They are dressed in black crape and their heads are shaved. Smiling, amiable, full of excuses, they offer us their hands, and we follow, with our feet bare like theirs, to the interior of their mysterious dwelling, through a series of empty rooms spread with mats of the most unimpeachable whiteness. The successive halls are separated one from the other only by bamboo curtains of exquisite delicacy, caught back by tassels and cords of red silk.

The whole wainscoting of the interior is of the same wood, of a pale yellow shade made with extreme nicety, without the least ornament, the least carving; everything seems new and unused, as if it had never been touched by human hand. At distant intervals in this studied bareness, costly little stools, marvellously inlaid, uphold some antique bronze monster or a vase of flowers; on the walls hang a few masterly sketches, vaguely tinted in Indian ink, drawn upon strips of gray paper most accurately cut but without the slightest attempt at a frame. This is all: not a seat, not a cushion, not a scrap of furniture. It is the very acme of studied simplicity, of elegance made out of nothing, of the most immaculate and incredible cleanliness. And while following the bonzes through this long suite of empty halls, we are struck by their contrast with the overflow of knickknacks scattered about our rooms in France, and we take a sudden dislike to the profusion and crowding delighted in at home.

The spot where this silent march of barefooted folk comes to an end, the spot where we are to seat ourselves in the delightful coolness of a semi- darkness, is an interior veranda opening upon an artificial site. We might suppose it the bottom of a well; it is a miniature garden no bigger than the opening of an oubliette, overhung on all sides by the crushing height of the mountain and receiving from on high but the dim light of dreamland. Nevertheless, here is simulated a great natural ravine in all its wild grandeur: here are caverns, abrupt rocks, a torrent, a cascade, islands. The trees, dwarfed by a Japanese process of which we have not the secret, have tiny little leaves on their decrepit and knotty branches. A pervading hue of the mossy green of antiquity harmonizes all this medley, which is undoubtedly centuries old.

Families of goldfish swim round and round in the clear water, and tiny tortoises (jumpers probably) sleep upon the granite islands, which are of the same color as their own gray shells.

There are even blue dragon-flies which have ventured to descend, heaven knows whence, and alight with quivering wings upon the miniature water- lilies.

Our friends the bonzes, notwithstanding an unctuousness of manner thoroughly ecclesiastical, are very ready to laugh—a simple, pleased, childish laughter;

plump, chubby, shaven and shorn, they dearly love our French liqueurs and know how to take a joke.

We talk first of one thing and then another. To the tranquil music of their little cascade, I launch out before them with phrases of the most erudite Japanese, I try the effect of a few tenses of verbs: 'desideratives, concessives, hypothetics in ba'. While they chant they despatch the affairs of the church: the order of services sealed with complicated seals for inferior pagodas situated in the neighborhood; or trace little prayers with a cunning paint-brush, as medical remedies to be swallowed like pills by invalids at a distance. With their white and dimpled hands they play with a fan as cleverly as any woman, and when we have tasted different native drinks, flavored with essences of flowers, they bring up as a finish a bottle of Benedictine or Chartreuse, for they appreciate the liqueurs composed by their Western colleagues.

When they come on board to return our visits, they by no means disdain to fasten their great round spectacles on their flat noses in order to inspect the profane drawings in our illustrated papers, the 'Vie Parisienne' for instance. And it is even with a certain complacency that they let their fingers linger upon the pictures representing women.

The religious ceremonies in their great temple are magnificent, and to one of these we are now invited. At the sound of the gong they make their entrance before the idols with a stately ritual; twenty or thirty priests officiate in gala costumes, with genuflections, clapping of hands and movements to and fro, which look like the figures of some mystic quadrille.

But for all that, let the sanctuary be ever so immense and imposing in its sombre gloom, the idols ever so superb, all seems in Japan but a mere semblance of grandeur. A hopeless pettiness, an irresistible effect the ludicrous, lies at the bottom of all things.

And then the congregation is not conducive to thoughtful contemplation, for among it we usually discover some acquaintance: my mother-in-law, or a cousin, or the woman from the china-shop who sold us a vase only yesterday. Charming little mousmes, monkeyish-looking old ladies enter with their smoking-boxes, their gayly daubed parasols, their curtseys, their little cries and exclamations; prattling, complimenting one another, full of restless movement, and having the greatest difficulty in maintaining a serious demeanor.

CHAPTER XLI

AN UNEXPECTED CALL

September 3d.

My little Chrysantheme for the first time visited me on board-ship to day, chaperoned by Madame Prune, and followed by my youngest sister in- law, Mademoiselle La Neige. These ladies had the tranquil manners of the highest gentility. In my cabin is a great Buddha on his throne, and before him is a lacquer tray, on which my faithful sailor servant places any small change he may find in the pockets of my clothes. Madame Prune, whose mind is much swayed by mysticism, at once supposed herself before a regular altar; in the gravest manner possible she addressed a brief prayer to the god; then drawing out her purse (which, according to custom, was attached to her sash behind her back, along with her little pipe and tobacco-pouch), placed a pious offering in the tray, while executing a low curtsey.

They were on their best behavior throughout the visit. But when the moment of departure came, Chrysantheme, who would not go away without seeing Yves, asked for him with a thinly veiled persistency which was remarkable. Yves, for whom I then sent, made himself particularly charming to her, so much so that this time I felt a shade of more serious annoyance; I even asked myself whether the laughably pitiable ending, which I had hitherto vaguely foreseen, might not, after all, soon break upon us.

CHAPTER XLII

AN ORIENTAL VISION

September 4th.

Yesterday I encountered, in an ancient and ruined quarter of the town, a perfectly exquisite mousme, charmingly dressed; a fresh touch of color against the sombre background of decayed buildings.

I met her at the farthest end of Nagasaki, in the most ancient part of the town. In this region are trees centuries old, antique temples of Buddha, of Amiddah, of Benten, or Kwanon, with steep and pompous roofs; monsters carved in granite sit there in courtyards silent as the grave, where the grass grows between the stones. This deserted quarter is traversed by a narrow torrent running in a deep channel, across which are thrown little curved bridges with granite balustrades eaten away by lichen. All the objects there wear the strange grimace, the quaint arrangement familiar to us in the most antique Japanese drawings.

I walked through it all at the burning hour of midday, and saw not a soul, unless, indeed, through the open windows of the bonze-houses, I caught sight of some few priests, guardians of tombs or sanctuaries, taking their siesta under dark-blue gauze nets.

Suddenly this little mousme appeared, a little above me, just at the point of the arch of one of these bridges carpeted with gray moss; she was in full sunshine, and stood out in brilliant clearness, like a fairy vision, against the background of old black temples and deep shadows. She was holding her robe together with one hand, gathering it close round her ankles to give herself an air of greater slimness. Over her quaint little head, her round umbrella with its thousand ribs threw a great halo of blue and red, edged with black, and an oleander-tree full of flowers, growing among the stones of the bridge, spread its glory beside her, bathed, like herself, in the sunshine. Behind this youthful figure and this flowering shrub all was blackness. Upon the pretty red and blue parasol great white letters formed this inscription, much used among the mousmes, and which I have learned to recognize: 'Stop! clouds, to see her pass!' And it was really worth the trouble to stop and look at this exquisite little person, of a type so ideally Japanese.

However, it will not do to stop too long and be ensnared—it would only be another delusion. A doll like the rest, evidently, an ornament for a china shelf, and nothing more. While I gaze at her, I say to myself that Chrysantheme, appearing in this same place, with this dress, this play of light, and this aureole of sunshine, would produce just as delightful an effect.

For Chrysantheme is pretty, there can be no doubt about it. Yesterday evening, in fact, I positively admired her. It was quite night; we were returning with the usual escort of little married couples like ourselves, from the inevitable tour of the tea-houses and bazaars. While the other mousmes walked along hand in hand, adorned with new silver topknots which they had succeeded in having presented to them, and amusing themselves with playthings, she, pleading fatigue, followed, half reclining, in a djin carriage. We had placed beside her great bunches of flowers destined to fill our vases, late iris and long-stemmed lotus, the last of the season, already smelling of autumn. And it was really very pretty to see this Japanese girl in her little car, lying carelessly among all these water-flowers, lighted by gleams of ever-changing colors, as they chanced from the lanterns we met or passed. If, on the evening of my arrival in Japan, any one had pointed her out to me, and said: "That shall be your mousme," there can not be a doubt I should have been charmed. In reality, however, I am not charmed; it is only Chrysantheme, always Chrysantheme, nothing but Chrysantheme: a mere plaything to laugh at, a little creature of finical forms and thoughts, with whom the agency of M. Kangourou has supplied me.

CHAPTER XLIII

THE CATS AND THE DOLLS

The water used for drinking in our house, for making tea, and for lesser washing purposes, is kept in large white china tubs, decorated with paintings representing blue fish borne along by a swift current through distorted rushes. In order to keep them cool, the tubs are kept out of doors on Madame Prune's roof, at a place where we can, from the top of our projecting balcony, easily reach them by stretching out an arm. A real godsend for all the thirsty cats in the neighborhood, on warm summer nights, is this corner of the roof with our gayly painted tubs, and it proves a delightful trysting-place for them, after all their caterwauling and long solitary rambles on the tops of the walls.

I had thought it my duty to warn Yves the first time he wished to drink this water.

"Oh!" he replied, rather surprised, "cats, do you say? But they are not dirty!"

On this point Chrysantheme and I agree with him: we do not consider cats unclean animals, and we do not object to drink after them.

Yves considers Chrysantheme much in the same light. "She is not dirty, either," he says; and he willingly drinks after her, out of the same cup, putting her in the same category with the cats.

These china tubs are one of the daily preoccupations of our household: in the evening, when we return from our walk, after the clamber up, which makes us thirsty, and Madame L'Heure's waffles, which we have been eating to beguile the way, we always find them empty. It seems impossible for Madame Prune, or Mademoiselle Oyouki, or their young servant, Mademoiselle Dede,— [Dede-San means "Miss Young Girl," a very common name.]—to have forethought enough to fill them while it is still daylight. And when we are late in returning home, these three ladies are asleep, so we are obliged to attend to the business ourselves.

We must therefore open all the closed doors, put on our boots, and go down into the garden to draw water.

As Chrysantheme would die of fright all alone in the dark, in the midst of the trees and buzzing of insects, I am obliged to accompany her to the well. For this expedition we require a light, and must seek among the quantity of lanterns purchased at Madame Tres-Propre's booth, which have been thrown night after night into the bottom of one of our little paper closets; but alas, all the candles are burned down! I thought as much! Well, we must resolutely take the first lantern to hand, and stick a fresh candle on the iron point at the bottom; Chrysantheme puts forth all her strength, the candle splits, breaks; the mousme pricks her fingers, pouts and whimpers. Such is the inevitable scene that takes place every evening, and delays our retiring to rest under the dark-blue gauze net for a good quarter of an hour; while the cicalas on the roof seem to mock us with their ceaseless song.

All this, which I should find amusing in any one else,—any one I loved —irritates me in her.

CHAPTER XLIV

TENDER MINISTRATIONS

September 11th.

A week has passed very quietly, during which I have written nothing.

By degrees I am becoming accustomed to my Japanese household, to the strangeness of the language, costumes, and faces. For the last three weeks no letters have arrived from Europe; they have no doubt miscarried, and their absence contributes, as is usually the case, to throw a veil of oblivion over the past.

Every day, therefore, I climb up to my villa, sometimes by beautiful starlit nights, sometimes through downpours of rain. Every morning as the sound of Madame Prune's chanted prayer rises through the reverberating air, I awake and go down toward the sea, by grassy pathways full of dew.

The chief occupation in Japan seems to be a perpetual hunt after curios. We sit down on the mattings, in the antique-sellers' little booths, taking a cup of tea with the salesmen, and rummage with our own hands in the cupboards and chests, where many a fantastic piece of old rubbish is huddled away. The bargaining, much discussed, is laughingly carried on for several days, as if we were trying to play off some excellent little practical joke upon each other.

I really make a sad abuse of the adjective little; I am quite aware of it, but how can I do otherwise? In describing this country, the temptation is great to use it ten times in every written line. Little, finical; affected,—all Japan is contained, both physically and morally, in these three words.

My purchases are accumulating in my little wood and paper house; but how much more Japanese it really was, in its bare emptiness, such as M. Sucre and Madame Prune had conceived it. There are now many lamps of sacred symbolism hanging from the ceiling; many stools and many vases, as many gods and goddesses as in a pagoda.

There is even a little Shintoist altar, before which Madame Prune has not been able to restrain her feelings, and before which she has fallen down and chanted her prayers in her bleating, goat-like voice:

"Wash me clean from all my impurity, O Ama-Terace-Omi-Kami! as one washes away uncleanness in the river of Kamo."

Alas for poor Ama-Terace-Omi-Kami to have to wash away the impurities of Madame Prune!

What a tedious and ungrateful task!!

Chrysantheme, who is a Buddhist, prays sometimes in the evening before lying down; although overcome with sleep, she prays clapping her hands before the largest of our gilded idols. But she smiles with a childish disrespect for her Buddha, as soon as her prayer is ended. I know that she has also a certain veneration for her Ottokes (the spirits of her ancestors), whose rather sumptuous altar is set up at the house of her mother, Madame Renoncule. She asks for their blessings, for fortune and wisdom.

Who can fathom her ideas about the gods, or about death? Does she possess a soul? Does she think she has one? Her religion is an obscure chaos of theogonies as old as the world, treasured up out of respect for ancient customs; and of more recent ideas about the blessed final annihilation, imported from India by saintly Chinese missionaries at the epoch of our Middle Ages. The bonzes themselves are puzzled; what a muddle, therefore, must not all this become, when jumbled together in the childish brain of a sleepy mousme!

Two very insignificant episodes have somewhat attached me to her—(bonds of this kind seldom fail to draw closer in the end). The first occasion was as follows:

Madame Prune one day brought forth a relic of her gay youth, a tortoise- shell comb of rare transparency, one of those combs that it is good style to place on the summit of the head, lightly poised, hardly stuck at all in the hair, with all the teeth showing. Taking it out of a pretty little lacquered box, she held it up in the air and blinked her eyes, looking through it at the sky—a bright summer sky—as one does to examine the quality of a precious stone.

"Here is," she said, "an object of great value that you should offer to your little wife."

My mousme, very much taken by it, admired the clearness of the comb and its graceful shape.

The lacquered box, however, pleased me more. On the cover was a wonderful painting in gold on gold, representing a field of rice, seen very close, on a windy day; a tangle of ears and grass beaten down and twisted by a terrible squall; here and there, between the distorted stalks, the muddy earth of the rice-swamp was visible; there were even little pools of water, produced by bits of the transparent lacquer on which tiny particles of gold seemed to float about like chaff in a thick liquid; two or three insects, which required a microscope to be well seen, were clinging in a terrified manner to the rushes, and the whole picture was no larger than a woman's hand.

As for Madame Prune's comb, I confess it left me indifferent, and I turned a deaf ear, thinking it very insignificant and expensive. Then Chrysantheme answered, mournfully:

"No, thank you, I don't want it; take it away, dear Madame Prune."

And at the same time she heaved a deep sigh, full of meaning, which plainly said:

"He is not so fond of me as all that.—Useless to bother him."

I immediately made the wished-for purchase.

Later when Chrysantheme will have become an old monkey like Madame Prune, with her black teeth and long orisons, she, in her turn, will retail that comb to some fine lady of a fresh generation.

On another occasion the sun had given me a headache; I lay on the floor resting my head on my snake-skin pillow. My eyes were dim; and everything appeared to turn around: the open veranda, the big expanse of luminous evening sky, and a variety of kites hovering against its background. I felt myself vibrating painfully to the rhythmical sound of the cicalas which filled the atmosphere.

She, crouching by my side, strove to relieve me by a Japanese process, pressing with all her might on my temples with her little thumbs and turning them rapidly around, as if she were boring a hole with a gimlet. She had become quite hot and red over this hard work, which procured me real comfort, something similar to the dreamy intoxication of opium.

Then, anxious and fearful lest I should have an attack of fever, she rolled into a pellet and thrust into my mouth a very efficacious prayer written on rice-paper, which she had kept carefully in the lining of one of her sleeves.

Well, I swallowed that prayer without a smile, not wishing to hurt her feelings or shake her funny little faith.

CHAPTER XLV

TWO FAIR ARISTOCRATS

Today, Yves, my mousmé and I went to the best photographer in Nagasaki, to be taken in a group. We shall send the picture to France. Yves laughs as he thinks of his wife's astonishment when she sees Chrysanthème's little face between us, and he wonders how he shall explain it to her.

"I shall just say it is one of your friends, that's all!" he says to me.

In Japan there are many photographers like our own, with this difference, that they are Japanese, and inhabit Japanese houses. The one we intend to honor to-day carries on his business in the suburbs, in that ancient quarter of big trees and gloomy pagodas where, the other day, I met the pretty little mousmé. His signboard, written in several languages, is posted against a wall on the edge of the little torrent which, rushing down from the green mountain above, is crossed by many a curved bridge of old granite and lined on either side with light bamboos or oleanders in full bloom.

It is astonishing and puzzling to find a photographer perched there, in the very heart of old Japan.

We have come at the wrong moment; there is a file of people at the door. Long rows of djins' cars are stationed there, awaiting the customers they have brought, who will all have their turn before us. The runners, naked and tattooed, their hair carefully combed in sleek bands and shiny chignons, are chatting, smoking little pipes, or bathing their muscular legs in the fresh water of the torrent.

The courtyard is irreproachably Japanese, with its lanterns and dwarf trees. But the studio where one poses might be in Paris or Pontoise; the self-same chair in "old oak," the same faded "poufs," plaster columns, and pasteboard rocks.

The people who are being photographed at this moment are two ladies of quality, evidently mother and daughter, who are sitting together for a cabinet-size portrait, with accessories of the time of Louis XV. A strange group this, the first great ladies of this country I have seen so near, with their long, aristocratic faces, dull, lifeless, almost gray by dint of rice-powder, and their mouths painted heart-shape in vivid carmine. Withal they have an undeniable look of good breeding that strongly impresses us, notwithstanding the intrinsic differences of race and acquired notions.

They scanned Chrysantheme with a look of obvious scorn, although her costume was as ladylike as their own. For my part, I could not take my eyes off these two creatures; they captivated me like incomprehensible things that one never had seen before. Their fragile bodies, outlandishly graceful in posture, are lost in stiff materials and redundant sashes, of which the ends droop like tired wings. They make me think, I know not why, of great rare insects; the extraordinary patterns on their garments have something of the dark motley of night-moths. Above all, I ponder over the mystery of their tiny slits of eyes, drawn back and up so far that the tight-drawn lids can hardly open; the mystery of their expression, which seems to denote inner thoughts of a silly, vague, complacent absurdity, a world of ideas absolutely closed to ourselves. And I think as I gaze at them: "How far we are from this Japanese people! how totally dissimilar are our races!"

We are compelled to let several English sailors pass before us, decked out in their white drill clothes, fresh, fat, and pink, like little sugar figures, who attitudinize in a sheepish manner around the shafts of the columns.

At last it is our turn; Chrysantheme settles herself slowly in a very affected style, turning in the points of her toes as much as possible, according to the fashion.

And on the negative shown to us we look like a supremely ridiculous little family drawn up in a line by a common photographer at a fair.

CHAPTER XLVI

GRAVE SUSPICIONS

September 13th.

Tonight Yves is off duty three hours earlier than I; occasionally this happens, according to the arrangement of the watches. At those times he lands first, and goes up to wait for me at Diou-djen-dji.

From the deck I can see him through my glass, climbing up the green mountain-path; he walks with a brisk, rapid step, almost running; what a hurry he seems in to rejoin little Chrysantheme!

When I arrive, about nine o'clock, I find him seated on the floor, in the middle of my rooms, with naked torso (this is a sufficiently proper costume for private life here, I admit). Around him are grouped Chrysantheme, Oyouki, and Mademoiselle Dede the maid, all eagerly rubbing his back with little blue towels decorated with storks and humorous subjects.

Good heavens! what can he have been doing to be so hot, and to have put himself in such a state?

He tells me that near our house, a little farther up the mountain, he has discovered a fencing-gallery: that till nightfall he had been engaged in a fencing-bout against Japanese, who fought with two-handed swords, springing like cats, as is the custom of their country. With his French method of fencing, he had given them a good drubbing. Upon which, with many a low bow, they had shown him their admiration by bringing him a quantity of nice little iced things to drink. All this combined had thrown him into a fearful perspiration.

Ah, very well! Nevertheless, this did not quite explain to me!

He is delighted with his evening; intends to go and amuse himself every day by beating them; he even thinks of taking pupils.

Once his back is dried, all together, the three mousmes and himself, play at Japanese pigeon-vole. Really I could not wish for anything more innocent, or more correct in every respect.

Charles N—— and Madame Jonquille, his wife, arrived unexpectedly about ten o'clock. (They were wandering about in the dark shrubberies in our neighborhood, and, seeing our lights, came up to us.)

They intend to finish the evening at the tea-house of the toads, and they try to induce us to go and drink some iced sherbets with them. It is at least an hour's walk from here, on the other side of the town, halfway up the hill, in the gardens of the large pagoda dedicated to Osueva; but they stick to their idea, pretending that in this clear night and bright moonlight we shall have a lovely view from the terrace of the temple.

Lovely, I have no doubt, but we had intended going to bed. However, be it so, let us go with them.

We hire five djins and five cars down below, in the principal street, in front of Madame Tres-Propre's shop, who, for this late expedition, chooses for us her largest round lanterns-big, red balloons, decorated with starfish, seaweed, and green sharks.

It is nearly eleven o'clock when we make our start. In the central quarters the virtuous Nipponese are already closing their little booths, putting out their lamps, shutting the wooden framework, drawing their paper panels.

Farther on, in the old-fashioned suburban streets, all is shut up long ago, and our carts roll on through the black night. We cry out to our djins: "Ayakou! ayakou!" ("Quick! quick!")and they run as hard as they can, uttering little shrieks, like merry animals full of wild gayety. We rush like a whirlwind through the darkness, all five in Indian file, dashing and jolting over the old, uneven flagstones, dimly lighted up by our red balloons fluttering at the end of their bamboo stems. From time to time some Japanese, night-capped in his blue kerchief, opens a window to see who these noisy madcaps can be, dashing by so rapidly and so late. Or else some faint glimmer, thrown by us on our passage, discovers the hideous smile of a large stone animal seated at the gate of a pagoda.

At last we arrive at the foot of Osueva's temple, and, leaving our djins with our little gigs, we clamber up the gigantic steps, completely deserted at this hour of the night.

Chrysantheme, who always likes to play the part of a tired little girl, of a spoiled and pouting child, ascends slowly between Yves and myself, clinging to our arms.

Jonquille, on the contrary, skips up like a bird, amusing herself by counting the endless steps.

She lays a great stress on the accentuations, as if to make the numbers sound even more droll.

A little silver aigrette glitters in her beautiful black coiffure; her delicate and graceful figure seems strangely fantastic, and the darkness that envelops us conceals the fact that her face is quite ugly, and almost without eyes.

This evening Chrysantheme and Jonquille really look like little fairies; at certain moments the most insignificant Japanese have this appearance, by dint of whimsical elegance and ingenious arrangement.

The granite stairs, imposing, deserted, uniformly gray under the nocturnal sky, appear to vanish into the empty space above us, and, when we turn round, to disappear in the depths beneath, to fall into the abyss with the dizzy rapidity of a dream. On the sloping steps the black shadows of the gateways through which we must pass stretch out indefinitely; and the shadows, which seem to be broken at each projecting step, look like the regular creases of a fan. The porticoes stand up separately, rising one above another; their wonderful shapes are at once remarkably simple and studiously affected; their outlines stand out sharp and distinct, having nevertheless the vague appearance of all very large objects in the pale moonlight. The curved architraves rise at each extremity like two menacing horns, pointing upward toward the far-off blue canopy of the star-spangled sky, as if they would communicate to the gods the knowledge they have acquired in the depths of their foundations from the earth, full of sepulchres and death, which surrounds them.

We are, indeed, a very small group, lost now in the immensity of the colossal acclivity as we move onward, lighted partly by the wan moon, partly by the red lanterns we hold in our hands, floating at the ends of their long sticks.

A deep silence reigns in the precincts of the temple, even the sound of insects is hushed as we ascend. A sort of reverence, a kind of religious fear steals over us, and, at the same moment, a delicious coolness suddenly pervades the air, and passes over us.

On entering the courtyard above, we feel a little daunted. Here we find the horse in jade, and the china turrets. The enclosing walls make it the more gloomy, and our arrival seems to disturb I know not what mysterious council held between the spirits of the air and the visible symbols that are there, chimeras and monsters illuminated by the blue rays of the moon.

We turn to the left, and go through the terraced gardens, to reach the tea-house of the toads, which this evening is our goal; we find it shut up—I expected as much—closed and dark, at this hour! We drum all together on the door; in the most coaxing tones we call by name the waiting-maids we know so well: Mademoiselle Transparente, Mademoiselle Etoile, Mademoiselle Rosee-matinale, and Mademoiselle Margueritereine. Not an answer. Good-by, perfumed sherbets and frosted beans!

In front of the little archery-house our mousmes suddenly jump aside, terrified, declaring that there is a dead body on the ground. Yes, indeed, some one is lying there. We cautiously examine the place by the light of our red balloons, carefully held out at arm's length for fear of this dead man. It is only the marksman, he who on the 4th of July chose such magnificent arrows for Chrysantheme; and he sleeps, good man! with his chignon somewhat dishevelled, a sound sleep, which it would be cruel to disturb.

Let us go to the end of the terrace, contemplate the harbor at our feet, and then return home. To-night the harbor looks like only a dark and sinister rent, which the moonbeams can not fathom—a yawning crevasse opening into the very bowels of the earth, at the bottom of which lie faint, small glimmers, an assembly of glowworms in a ditch—the lights of the different vessels lying at anchor.

CHAPTER XLVII

A MIDNIGHT ALARM

It is the middle of the night, perhaps about two o'clock in the morning. Our lamps are burning somewhat dimly before our placid idols. Chrysantheme wakes me suddenly, and I turn to look at her: she has raised herself on one arm, and her face expresses the most intense terror; she makes a sign, without daring to speak, that some one or something is near, creeping up to us. What ill-timed visit is this? A feeling of fear gains possession of me also. I have a rapid impression of some great unknown danger, in this isolated spot, in this strange country of which I do not even yet comprehend the inhabitants and the mysteries. It must be something very frightful to hold her there, rooted to the spot, half dead with fright, she who does comprehend all these things.

It seems to be outside; it is coming from the garden; with trembling hand she indicates to me that it will come through the veranda, over Madame Prune's roof. Certainly, I hear faint noises, and they do approach us.

I suggest to her

"Neko-San?" ("It is Messieurs the cats?")

"No!" she replies, still terrified, and in an alarmed tone.

"Bakemono-Sama?" ("Is it my lords the ghosts?") I have already the Japanese habit of expressing myself with excessive politeness.

"No! 'Dorobo'!" ("Thieves!")

Thieves! Ah! this is better; I much prefer this to a visit such as I have just been dreading in the sudden awakening from sleep: from ghosts or spirits of the dead; thieves, that is to say, worthy fellows very much alive, and having, undoubtedly, inasmuch as they are Japanese thieves, faces of the most meritorious oddity. I am not in the least frightened, now that I know precisely what to expect, and we will immediately set to work to ascertain the truth, for something is certainly moving on Madame Prune's roof; some one is walking upon it.

I open one of our wooden panels and look out.

I can see only a vast expanse, calm, peaceful, and exquisite under the full brilliance of the moonlight; sleeping Japan, lulled by the sonorous song of the grasshoppers, is charming indeed to-night, and the free, pure air is delicious.

Chrysantheme, half hidden behind my shoulder, listens tremblingly, peering forward to examine the gardens and the roofs with dilated eyes like a frightened cat. No, nothing! not a thing moves. Here and there are a few strangely substantial shadows, which at first glance were not easy to explain, but which turn out to be real shadows, thrown by bits of wall, by boughs of trees, and which preserve an extremely reassuring stillness. Everything seems absolutely tranquil, and profound silence reigns in the dreamy vagueness which moonlight sheds over all.

Nothing; nothing to be seen anywhere. It was Messieurs the cats after all, or perhaps my ladies the owls; sounds increase in volume in the most amazing manner at night, in this house of ours.

Let us close the panel again carefully, as a measure of prudence, and then light a lantern and go downstairs to see whether there may be any one hidden in corners, and whether the doors are tightly shut; in short, to reassure Chrysantheme we will go the round of the house.

Behold us, then, on tiptoe, searching together every hole and corner of the house, which, to judge by its foundations, must be very ancient, notwithstanding the fragile appearance of its panels of white paper. It contains the blackest of cavities, little vaulted cellars with worm-eaten beams; cupboards for rice which smell of mould and decay; mysterious hollows where lies accumulated the dust of centuries. In the middle of the night, and during a hunt for thieves, this part of the house, as yet unknown to me, has an ugly look.

Noiselessly we step across the apartment of our landlord and landlady. Chrysantheme drags me by the hand, and I allow myself to be led. There they are, sleeping in a row under their blue gauze tent, lighted by the night-lamps burning before the altars of their ancestors. Ha! I observe that they are arranged in an order which might give rise to gossip. First comes Mademoiselle Oyouki, very taking in her attitude of rest! Then Madame Prune, who sleeps with her mouth wide open, showing her rows of blackened teeth; from her throat arises an intermittent sound like the grunting of a sow. Oh! poor Madame Prune! how hideous she is!! Next, M. Sucre, a mere mummy for the time being. And finally, at his side, last of the row, is their servant, Mademoiselle Dede!

The gauze hanging over them throws reflections as of the sea upon them; one might suppose them victims drowned in an aquarium. And withal the sacred lamps, the altar crowded with strange Shintoist symbols, give a mock religious air to this family tableau.

'Honi soit qui mal y pense', but why is not that maidservant rather laid by the side of her mistresses? Now, when we on the floor above offer our hospitality to Yves, we are careful to place ourselves under our mosquito-net in a more correct style!

One corner, which as a last resort we inspect, inspires me with a certain amount of apprehension. It is a low, mysterious loft, against the door of which is stuck, as a thing no longer wanted, a very old, pious image Kwanon with the thousand arms, and Kwanon with the horses' head, seated among clouds and flames, both horrible to behold with their spectral grins.

We open the door, and Chrysantheme starts back uttering a fearful cry. I should have thought the robbers were there, had I not seen a little gray creature, rapid and noiseless, rush by her and disappear; a young rat that had been eating rice on the top of a shelf, and, in its alarm, had dashed in her face.

CHAPTER XLVIII

UNUSUAL HOSPITALITY

September 16th.

Yves has let fall his silver whistle in the ocean, the whistle so absolutely indispensable for the manoeuvres; and we search the town all day long, followed by Chrysantheme and Mesdemoiselles La Neige and La Lune, her sisters, in the endeavor to find another.

It is, however, very difficult to find such a thing in Nagasaki; above all, very difficult to explain in Japanese what is a sailor's whistle of the traditional shape, curved, and with a little ball at the end to modulate the trills and the various sounds of official orders. For three hours we are sent from shop to shop; at each one they pretend to understand perfectly what is wanted and trace on tissue-paper, with a paint-brush, the addresses of the shops where we shall without fail meet with what we require. Away we go, full of hope, only to encounter some fresh mystification, till our breathless djins get quite bewildered.

They understand admirably that we want a thing that will make a noise, music, in short; thereupon they offer us instruments of every, and of the most unexpected, shape—squeakers for Punch-and-Judy voices, dog-whistles, trumpets. Each time it is something more and more absurd, so that at last we are overcome with uncontrollable fits of laughter. Last of all, an aged Japanese optician, who assumes a most knowing air, a look of sublime wisdom, goes off to forage in his back shop, and brings to light a steam fog-horn, a relict from some wrecked steamer.

After dinner, the chief event of the evening is a deluge of rain, which takes us by surprise as we leave the teahouses, on our return from our fashionable stroll. It so happened that we were a large party, having with us several mousmé guests, and from the moment that the rain began to fall from the skies, as if out of a watering-pot turned upside down, the band became disorganized. The mousmes run off, with bird-like cries, and take refuge under doorways, in the shops, under the hoods of the djins.

Then, before long—when the shops shut up in haste, when the emptied streets are flooded, and almost black, and the paper lanterns, piteous objects, wet through and extinguished—I find myself, I know not how it happens, flattened against a wall, under the projecting eaves, alone in the company of Mademoiselle Fraise, my cousin, who is crying bitterly because her fine robe is wet through. And in the noise of the rain, which is still falling, and splashing everything with the spouts and gutters, which in the darkness plaintively murmur like running streams, the town appears to me suddenly an abode of the gloomiest sadness.

The shower is soon over, and the mousmes come out of their holes like so many mice; they look for one another, call one another, and their little voices take the singular, melancholy, dragging inflections they assume whenever they have to call from afar.

"Hi! Mademoiselle Lu-u-u-u-une!"

"Hi! Madame Jonqui-i-i-i-ille!"

They shout from one to another their outlandish names, prolonging them indefinitely in the now silent night, in the reverberations of the damp air after the great summer rain.

At length they are all collected and united again, these tiny personages with narrow eyes and no brains, and we return to Diou-djen-dji all wet through.

For the third time, we have Yves sleeping beside us under our blue tent.

There is a great noise shortly after midnight in the apartment beneath us: our landlord's family have returned from a pilgrimage to a far- distant temple of the Goddess of Grace. (Although Madame Prune is a Shintoist, she reveres this deity, who, scandal says, watched over her youth.) A moment after, Mademoiselle Oyouki bursts into our room like a rocket, bringing, on a charming little tray, sweetmeats which have been blessed and bought at the gates of the temple yonder, on purpose for us, and which we must positively eat at once, before the virtue is gone out of them. Hardly rousing ourselves, we absorb these little edibles flavored with sugar and pepper, and return a great many sleepy thanks.

Yves sleeps quietly on this occasion, without dealing any blows to the floor or the panels with either fists or feet. He has hung his watch on one of the hands of our gilded idol in order to be more sure of seeing the hour at any time of the night, by the light of the sacred lamps. He gets up betimes in the morning, asking: "Well, did I behave properly?" and dresses in haste, preoccupied about duty and the roll-call.

Outside, no doubt, it is daylight already: through the tiny holes which time has pierced in our wooden panels, threads of morning light penetrate our chamber, and in the atmosphere of our room where night still lingers, they trace vague white rays. Soon, when the sun shall have risen, these rays will lengthen and become beautifully golden. The cocks and the cicalas make themselves heard, and now Madame Prune will begin her mystic drone.

Nevertheless, out of politeness for Yves-San, Chrysantheme lights a lantern and escorts him to the foot of the dark staircase. I even fancy that, on parting, I hear a kiss exchanged. In Japan this is of no consequence, I know; it is very usual, and quite admissible; no matter where one goes, in houses one enters for the first time, one is quite at liberty to kiss any mousme who may be present, without any notice being taken of it. But with regard to Chrysantheme, Yves is in a delicate position, and he ought to understand it better. I begin to feel uneasy about the hours they have so often spent together alone; and I make up my mind that this very day I will not play the spy upon them, but speak frankly to Yves, and make a clean breast of it.

Suddenly from below, clac! clac! two dry hands are clapped together; it is Madame Prune's warning to the Great Spirit. And immediately after her prayer breaks forth, soars upward in a shrill nasal falsetto, like a morning alarum when the hour for waking has come, the mechanical noise of a spring let go and running down.

".....The richest woman in the world! Cleansed from all my sins, O Ama-Terace-Omi-Kami! in the river of Kamo."

And this extraordinary bleating, hardly human, scatters and changes my ideas, which were very nearly clear at the moment I awoke.

CHAPTER XLIX

RUMORS OF DEPARTURE

September 15th.

Rumor of departure is in the air. Since yesterday there has been vague talk of our being sent to China, to the Gulf of Pekin; one of those rumors which spread, no one knows how, from one end of the ship to the other, two or three days before the official orders arrive, and which usually turn out tolerably correct. What will the last act of my little Japanese comedy be? the denouement, the separation? Will there be any touch of sadness on the part of my mousme, or on my own, just a tightening of the heartstrings at the moment of our final farewell? At this moment I can imagine nothing of the sort. And then the adieus of Yves and Chrysantheme, what will they be? This question preoccupies me more than all.

Nothing very definite has been learned as yet, but it is certain that, one way or another, our stay in Japan is drawing to a close. It is this, perhaps, which disposes me this evening to look more kindly on my surroundings. It is about six o'clock, after a day spent on duty, when I reach Diou-djen-dji. The evening sun, low in the sky, on the point of setting, pours into my room, and floods it with rays of red gold, lighting up the Buddhas and the great sheaves of quaintly arranged flowers in the antique vases. Here are assembled five or six little dolls, my neighbors, amusing themselves by dancing to the sound of Chrysantheme's guitar. And this evening I experienced a real charm in feeling that this dwelling and the woman who leads the dance are mine. On the whole, I have perhaps been unjust to this country; it seems to me that my eyes are at last opened to see it in its true light, that all my senses are undergoing a strange and abrupt transition. I suddenly have a better perception and appreciation of all the infinity of dainty trifles among which I live; of the fragile and studied grace of their forms, the oddity of their drawings, the refined choice of their colors.

I stretch myself upon the white mats; Chrysantheme, always eagerly attentive, brings me my pillow of serpent's-skin; and the smiling mousmes, with the interrupted rhythm of a while ago still running in their heads, move around me with measured steps.

Their immaculate socks with the separate great toes make no noise; nothing is heard, as they glide by, but a 'froufrou' of silken stuffs. I find them all pleasant to look upon; their dollish air pleases me now, and I fancy I have discovered what it is that gives it to them: it is not only their round, inexpressive faces with eyebrows far removed from the eyelids, but the excessive amplitude of their dress. With those huge sleeves, it might be supposed they have neither back nor shoulders; their delicate figures are lost in these wide robes, which float around what might be little marionettes without bodies at all, and which would slip to the ground of themselves were they not kept together midway, about where a waist should be, by the wide silken sashes—a very different comprehension of the art of dressing to ours, which endeavors as much as possible to bring into relief the curves, real or false, of the figure.

And then, how much I admire the flowers in our vases, arranged by Chrysantheme, with her Japanese taste, lotus-flowers, great, sacred flowers of a tender, veined rose color, the milky rose-tint seen on porcelain; they resemble, when in full bloom, great water-lilies, and when only in bud might be taken for long pale tulips. Their soft but rather cloying scent is added to that other indefinable odor of mousmes, of yellow race, of Japan, which is always and everywhere in the air. The late flowers of September, at this season very rare and expensive, grow on longer stems than the summer blooms; Chrysantheme has left them in their large aquatic leaves of a melancholy seaweed-green, and mingled with them tall, slight rushes. I look at them, and recall with some irony those great round bunches in the shape of cauliflowers, which our florists sell in France, wrapped in white lace-paper!

Still no letters from Europe, from any one. How things change, become effaced and forgotten! Here am I, accommodating myself to this finical Japan and dwindling down to its affected mannerism; I feel that my thoughts run in smaller grooves, my tastes incline to smaller things— things which suggest nothing greater than a smile. I am becoming used to tiny and ingenious furniture, to doll-like desks, to miniature bowls with which to play at dinner, to the immaculate monotony of the mats, to the finely finished simplicity of the white woodwork. I am even losing my Western prejudices; all my preconceived ideas are this evening evaporating and vanishing; crossing the garden I have courteously saluted M. Sucre, who was watering his dwarf shrubs and his deformed flowers; and Madame Prune appears to me a highly respectable old lady, in whose past there is nothing to criticise.

We shall take no walk to-night; my only wish is to remain stretched out where I am, listening to the music of my mousme's 'chamecen'.

Till now I have always used the word guitar, to avoid exotic terms, for the abuse of which I have been so reproached. But neither the word guitar nor mandolin suffices to designate this slender instrument with its long neck, the high notes of which are shriller than the voice of the grasshopper; and henceforth, I will write 'chamecen'.

I will also call my mousme Kikou, Kikou-San; this name suits her better than Chrysantheme, which, though translating the sense exactly, does not preserve the strange-sounding euphony of the original.

I therefore say to Kikou, my wife:

"Play, play on for me; I shall remain here all the evening and listen to you."

Astonished to find me in so amiable a mood, she requires pressing a little, and with almost a bitter curve of triumph and disdain upon her lips, she seats herself in the attitude of an idol, raises her long, dark-colored sleeves, and begins. The first hesitating notes are murmured faintly and mingle with the music of the insects humming outside, in the quiet air of the warm and golden twilight. First she plays slowly, a confused medley of fragments which she does not seem to remember perfectly, of which one waits for the finish and waits in vain; while the other girls giggle, inattentive, and regretful of their interrupted dance. She herself is absent, sulky, as if she were only performing a duty.

Then by degrees, little by little, the music becomes more animated, and the mousmes begin to listen. Now, tremblingly, it grows into a feverish rapidity, and her gaze has no longer the vacant stare of a doll. Then the music changes again; in it there is the sighing of the wind, the hideous laughter of ghouls; tears, heartrending plaints, and her dilated pupils seem to be directed inwardly in settled gaze on some indescribable Japanesery within her own soul.

I listen, lying there with eyes half shut, looking out between my drooping eyelids, which are gradually lowering, in involuntary heaviness, upon the enormous red sun dying away over Nagasaki. I have a somewhat melancholy feeling that my past life and all other places in the world are receding from my view and fading away. At this moment of nightfall I feel almost at home in this corner of Japan, amidst the gardens of this suburb. I never have had such an impression before.

CHAPTER L

A DOLLS' DUET

September 16th.

Seven o'clock in the evening. We shall not go down into Nagasaki tonight; but, like good Japanese citizens, remain in our lofty suburb.

In undress uniform we shall go, Yves and I, in a neighborly way, as far as the fencing-gallery, which is only two steps away, just above our villa, and almost abutting on our fresh and scented garden.

The gallery is closed already, and a little mousko, seated at the door, explains, with many low bows, that we come too late, all the amateurs are gone; we must come again tomorrow.

The evening is so mild and fine that we remain out of doors, following, without any definite purpose, the pathway which rises ever higher and higher, and loses itself at length in the solitary regions of the mountain among the upper peaks.

For an hour at least we wander on—an unintended walk—and finally find ourselves at a great height commanding an endless perspective lighted by the last gleams of daylight; we are in a desolate and mournful spot, in the midst of the little Buddhist cemeteries, which are scattered over the country in every direction.

We meet a few belated laborers, who are returning from the fields with bundles of tea upon their shoulders. These peasants have a half-savage air. They are half naked, too, or clothed only in long robes of blue cotton; as they pass, they salute us with humble bows.

No trees in this elevated region. Fields of tea alternate with tombs: old granite statues which represent Buddha in his lotus, or else old monumental stones on which gleam remains of inscriptions in golden letters. Rocks, brushwood, uncultivated spaces, surround us on all sides.

We meet no more passers-by, and the light is failing. We will halt for a moment, and then it will be time to turn our steps homeward.

But, close to the spot where we stand, a box of white wood provided with handles, a sort of sedan-chair, rests on the freshly disturbed earth, with its lotus of silvered paper, and the little incense-sticks, burning yet, by its side; clearly some one has been buried here this very evening.

I can not picture this personage to myself; the Japanese are so grotesque in life that it is almost impossible to imagine them in the calm majesty of death. Nevertheless, let us move farther on, we might disturb him; he is too recently dead, his presence unnerves us. We will go and seat ourselves on one of these other tombs, so unutterably ancient that there can no longer be anything within it but dust. And there, seated in the dying sunlight, while the valleys and plains of the earth below are already lost in shadow, we will talk together.

I wish to speak to Yves about Chrysantheme; it is indeed somewhat in view of this that I have persuaded him to sit down; but how to set about it without hurting his feelings, and without making myself ridiculous, I hardly know. However, the pure air playing round me up here, and the magnificent landscape spread beneath my feet, impart a certain serenity to my thoughts which makes me feel a contemptuous pity, both for my suspicions and the cause of them.

We speak, first of all, of the order for departure, which may arrive at any moment, for China or for France. Soon we shall have to leave this easy and almost amusing life, this Japanese suburb where chance has installed us, and our little house buried among flowers. Yves perhaps will regret all this more than I. I know that well enough; for it is the first time that any such interlude has broken the rude monotony of his hard-worked career. Formerly, when in an inferior rank, he was hardly more often on shore, in foreign countries, than the sea-gulls themselves; while I, from the very beginning, have been spoiled by residence in all sorts of charming spots, infinitely superior to this, in all sorts of countries, and the remembrance still haunts me pleasurably.

In order to discover how the land lies, I risk the remark:

"You will perhaps be more sorry to leave little Chrysantheme than I."

Silence reigns between us.

After which I go on, and, burning my ships, I add:

"You know, after all, if you have such a fancy for her, I haven't really married her; one can't really consider her my wife."

In great surprise he looks in my face.

"Not your wife, you say? But, by Jove, though, that's just it; she is your wife."

There is no need of many words at any time between us two; I know exactly now, by his tone, by his great good-humored smile, how the case stands; I understand all that lies in the little phrase: "That's just it, she is your wife." If she were not, well, then, he could not answer for what might happen—notwithstanding any remorse he might have in the depths of his heart, since he is no longer a bachelor and free as air, as in former days. But he considers her my wife, and she is sacred. I have the fullest faith in his word, and I experience a positive relief, a real joy, at finding my stanch Yves of bygone days. How could I have so succumbed to the demeaning influence of my surroundings as to suspect him even, and to invent for myself such a mean, petty anxiety?

We never shall even mention that doll again.

We remain up there very late, talking of other things, gazing at the immense depths below, at the valleys and mountains as they become, one by one, indistinct and lost in the deepening darkness. Placed as we are at an enormous height, in the wide, free atmosphere, we seem already to have quitted this miniature country, already to be freed from the impression of littleness which it has given us, and from the little links by which it was beginning to bind—us to itself.

Seen from such heights as these, all the countries of the globe bear a strong resemblance to one another; they lose the imprint made upon them by man, and by races; by all the atoms swarming on the surface.

As of old, in the Breton marshes, in the woods of Toulven, or at sea in the night-watches, we talk of all those things to which thoughts naturally revert in darkness; of ghosts, of spirits, of eternity, of the great hereafter, of chaos—and we entirely forget little Chrysantheme!

When we arrive at Diou-djen-dji in the starry night, the music of her 'chamecen', heard from afar, recalls to us her existence; she is studying some vocal duet with Mademoiselle Oyouki, her pupil.

I feel myself in very good humor this evening, and, relieved from my absurd suspicions about my poor Yves, am quite disposed to enjoy without reserve my last days in Japan, and to derive therefrom all the amusement possible.

Let us then repose ourselves on the dazzling white mats, and listen to the singular duet sung by those two mousmes: a strange musical medley, slow and mournful, beginning with two or three high notes, and descending at each couplet, in an almost imperceptible manner, into actual solemnity. The song keeps its dragging slowness; but the accompaniment, becoming more and more accentuated, is like the impetuous sound of a far- off hurricane. At the end, when these girlish voices, usually so soft, give out their hoarse and guttural notes, Chrysantheme's hands fly wildly and convulsively over the quivering strings. Both of them lower their heads, pout their underlips in the effort to bring out these astonishingly deep notes. And at these moments their little narrow eyes open, and seem to reveal an unexpected something, almost a soul, under these trappings of marionettes.

But it is a soul which more than ever appears to me of a different species from my own; I feel my thoughts to be as far removed from theirs as from the flitting conceptions of a bird, or the dreams of a monkey; I feel there is between them and myself a great gulf, mysterious and awful.

Other sounds of music, wafted to us from the distance, interrupt for a moment those of our mousmes. From the depths below, in Nagasaki, arises a sudden noise of gongs and guitars; we rush to the balcony of the veranda to hear it better.

It is a 'matsouri', a fete, a procession passing through the quarter which is not so virtuous as our own, so our mousmes tell us, with a disdainful toss of the head. Nevertheless, from the heights on which we dwell, seen thus in a bird's-eye view, by the uncertain light of the stars, this district has a singularly chaste air, and the concert going on therein, purified in its ascent from the depths of the abyss to our lofty altitudes, reaches us confusedly, a smothered, enchanted, enchanting sound.

Then it diminishes, and dies away into silence.

The two little friends return to their seats on the mats, and once more take up their melancholy duet. An orchestra, discreetly subdued but innumerable, of crickets and cicalas, accompanies them in an unceasing tremolo— the immense, far-reaching tremolo, which, gentle and eternal, never ceases in Japan.

CHAPTER LI

THE LAST DAY

September 17th

At the hour of siesta, a peremptory order arrives to start tomorrow for China, for Tche-fou (a terrible place, in the gulf of Pekin). Yves comes to wake me in my cabin to bring me the news.

"I must positively get leave to go on shore this evening," he says, while I endeavor to shake myself awake, "if it is only to help you to dismantle and pack up."

He gazes through my port-hole, raising his glance toward the green summits, in the direction of Diou-djen-dji and our echoing old cottage, hidden from us by a turn of the mountain.

It is very nice of him to wish to help me in my packing; but I think he counts also upon saying farewell to his little Japanese friends up there, and I really can not find fault with that.

He finishes his work, and does in fact obtain leave, without help from me, to go on shore at five o'clock, after drill and manoeuvres.

As for myself I start at once, in a hired sampan. In the vast flood of midday sunshine, to the quivering noise of the cicalas, I mount to Diou- djen-dji.

The paths are solitary, the plants are drooping in the heat. Here, however, is Madame Jonquille, taking the air in the bright, grasshoppers' sunshine, sheltering her dainty figure and her charming face under an enormous paper parasol, a huge circle, closely ribbed and fantastically striped.

She recognizes me from afar, and, laughing as usual, runs to meet me.

I announce our departure, and a tearful pout suddenly contracts her childish face. After all, does this news grieve her? Is she about to shed tears over it? No! it turns to a fit of laughter, a little nervous perhaps, but unexpected and disconcerting—dry and clear, pealing through the silence and warmth of the narrow paths, like a cascade of little mock pearls.

Ah, there indeed is a marriage-tie which will be broken without much pain! But she fills me with impatience, poor empty-headed linnet, with her laughter, and I turn my back upon her to continue my journey.

Above-stairs, Chrysantheme sleeps, stretched out on the floor; the house is wide open, and the soft mountain breeze rustles gently through it.

That same evening we had intended to give a tea-party, and by my orders flowers had already been placed in every nook and corner of the house. There were lotus in our vases, beautifully colored lotus, the last of the season, I verily believe. They must have been ordered from a special gardener, out yonder near the Great Temple, and they will cost me dear.

With a few gentle taps of a fan I awake my surprised mousme; and, curious to catch her first impressions, I announce my departure. She starts up, rubs her eyelids with the backs of her little hands, looks at me, and hangs her head: something like an expression of sadness passes in her eyes.

This little sinking at the heart is for Yves, no doubt!

The news spreads through the house.

Mademoiselle Oyouki dashes upstairs, with half a tear in each of her babyish eyes; kisses me with her full red lips, which always leave a wet ring on my cheek; then quickly draws from her wide sleeve a square of tissue-paper, wipes away her stealthy tears, blows her little nose, rolls the bit of paper in a ball, and throws it into the street on the parasol of a passer-by.

Then Madame Prune makes her appearance; in an agitated and discomposed manner she successively adopts every attitude expressive of dismay. What on earth is the matter with the old lady, and why does she keep getting closer and closer to me, till she is almost in my way?

It is wonderful to think of all that I still have to do this last day, and the endless drives I have to make to the old curiosity-shops, to my tradespeople, and to the packers.

Nevertheless, before my rooms are dismantled, I intend making a sketch of them, as I did formerly at Stamboul. It really seems to me as if all I do here is a bitter parody of all I did over there.

This time, however, it is not that I care for this dwelling; it is only because it is pretty and uncommon, and the sketch will be an interesting souvenir.

I fetch, therefore, a leaf out of my album, and begin at once, seated on the floor and leaning on my desk, ornamented with grasshoppers in relief, while behind me, very, very close to me, the three women follow the movements of my pencil with astonished attention. Japanese art being entirely conventional, they have never before seen any one draw from nature, and my style delights them. I may not perhaps possess the steady and nimble touch of M. Sucre, as he groups his charming storks, but I am master of a few notions of perspective which are wanting in him; and I have been taught to draw things as I see them, without giving them an ingeniously distorted and grimacing attitudes; and the three Japanese are amazed at the air of reality displayed in my sketch.

With little shrieks of admiration, they point out to one another the different things, as little by little their shape and form are outlined in black on my paper. Chrysantheme gazes at me with a new kind of interest "Anata itchiban!" she says (literally "Thou first!" meaning: "You are really quite wonderful!")

Mademoiselle Oyouki is carried away by her admiration, and exclaims, in a burst of enthusiasm:

"Anata bakari!" ("Thou alone!" that is to say: "There is no one like you in the world, all the rest are mere rubbish!")

Madame Prune says nothing, but I can see that she does not think the less; her languishing attitudes, her hand that at each moment gently touches mine, confirm the suspicions that her look of dismay a few moments ago awoke within me: evidently my physical charms speak to her imagination, which in spite of years has remained full of romance! I shall leave with the regret of having understood her too late!

Although the ladies are satisfied with my sketch, I am far from being so. I have put everything in its place most exactly, but as a whole, it has an ordinary, indifferent, French look which does not suit. The sentiment is not given, and I almost wonder whether I should not have done better to falsify the perspective—Japanese style—exaggerating to the very utmost the already abnormal outlines of what I see before me. And then the pictured dwelling lacks the fragile look and its sonority, that reminds one of a dry violin. In the pencilled delineation of the woodwork, the minute delicacy with which it is wrought is wanting; neither have I been able to give an idea of the extreme antiquity, the perfect cleanliness, nor the vibrating song of the cicalas that seems to have been stored away within it, in its parched-up fibres, during hundreds of summers. It does not convey, either, the impression this place gives of being in a far-off suburb, perched aloft among trees, above the drollest of towns. No, all this can not be drawn, can not be expressed, but remains undemonstrable, indefinable.

Having sent out our invitations, we shall, in spite of everything, give our tea-party this evening—a parting tea, therefore, in which we shall display as much pomp as possible. It is, moreover, rather my custom to wind up my exotic experiences with a fete; in other countries I have done the same.

Besides our usual set, we shall have my mother-in-law, my relatives, and all the mousmes of the neighborhood. But, by an extra Japanese refinement, we shall not admit a single European friend—not even the "amazingly tall" one. Yves alone shall be admitted, and even he shall be hidden away in a corner behind some flowers and works of art.

In the last glimmer of twilight, by the light of the first twinkling star, the ladies, with many charming curtseys, make their appearance. Our house is soon full of the little crouching women, with their tiny slit eyes vaguely smiling; their beautifully dressed hair shining like polished ebony; their fragile bodies lost in the many folds of the exaggerated, wide garments, that gape as if ready to drop from their little tapering backs and reveal the exquisite napes of their little necks.

Chrysantheme, with somewhat a melancholy air, and my mother-in-law, Madame Renoncule, with many affected graces busy themselves in the midst of the different groups, where ere long the miniature pipes are lighted. Soon there arises a murmuring sound of discreet laughter, expressing nothing, but having a pretty exotic ring about it, and then begins a harmony of tap! tap! tap!—sharp, rapid taps against the edges of the finely lacquered smoking-boxes. Pickled and spiced fruits are handed round on trays of quaint and varied shapes. Then transparent china teacups, no larger than half an egg-shell, make their appearance, and the ladies are offered a few drops of sugarless tea, poured out of toy kettles, or a sip of 'saki'—(a spirit made from rice which it is the custom to serve hot, in elegantly shaped vases, long-necked like a heron's throat).

Several mousmes execute, one after another, improvisations on the 'chamecen'. Others sing in sharp, high voices, hopping about continually, like cicalas in delirium.

Madame Prune, no longer able to make a mystery of the long-pent up feelings that agitate her, pays me the most marked and tender attentions, and begs my acceptance of a quantity of little souvenirs: an image, a little vase, a little porcelain goddess of the moon in Satsuma ware, a marvellously grotesque ivory figure;—I tremblingly follow her into the dark corners whither she calls me to give me these presents in tete- a-tete.

About nine o'clock, with a silken rustling, arrive the three geishas in vogue in Nagasaki: Mesdemoiselles Purete, Orange, and Printemps, whom I have hired at four dollars each—an enormous price in this country.

These three geishas are indeed the very same little creatures I heard singing on the rainy day of my arrival, through the thin panelling of the Garden of Flowers. But as I have now become thoroughly Japanized, today they appear to me more diminutive, less outlandish, and in no way mysterious. I treat them rather as dancers that I have hired, and the idea that I ever had thought of marrying one of them now makes me shrug my shoulders—as it formerly made M. Kangourou.

The excessive heat caused by the respiration of the mousmes and the burning lamps, brings out the perfume of the lotus, which fills the heavy-laden atmosphere; and the scent of camellia-oil, which the ladies use in profusion to make their hair glisten, is also strong in the room.

Mademoiselle Orange, the youngest geisha, tiny and dainty, her lips outlined with gilt paint, executes some delightful steps, donning the most extraordinary wigs and masks of wood or cardboard. She has masks imitating old, noble ladies which are valuable works of art, signed by well-known artists. She has also magnificent long robes, fashioned in the old style, with trains trimmed at the bottom with thick pads, in order to give to the movements of the costume something rigid and unnatural which, however, is becoming.

Now the soft balmy breezes blow through the room, from one veranda to the other, making the flames of the lamps flicker. They scatter the lotus flowers faded by the artificial heat, which, falling in pieces from every vase, sprinkle the guests with their pollen and large pink petals, looking like bits of broken, opal-colored glass.

The sensational piece, reserved for the end, is a trio on the 'chamecen', long and monotonous, that the geishas perform as a rapid pizzicato on the highest strings, very sharply struck. It sounds like the very quintessence, the paraphrase, the exasperation, if I may so call it, of the eternal buzz of insects, which issues from the trees, old roofs, old walls, from everything in fact, and which is the foundation of all Japanese sounds.

Half-past ten! The programme has been carried out, and the reception is over. A last general tap! tap! tap! the little pipes are stowed away in their chased sheaths, tied up in the sashes, and the mousmes rise to depart.

They light, at the end of short sticks, a quantity of red, gray, or blue lanterns, and after a series of endless bows and curtseys, the guests disperse in the darkness of the lanes and trees.

We also go down to the town, Yves, Chrysantheme, Oyouki and I—in order to conduct my mother-in-law, sisters-in-law, and my youthful aunt, Madame Nenufar, to their house.

We wish to take one last stroll together in our old familiar pleasure- haunts, to drink one more iced sherbet at the house of the Indescribable Butterflies, buy one more lantern at Madame Tres-Propre's, and eat some parting waffles at Madame L'Heure's!

I try to be affected, moved, by this leave-taking, but without success. In regard to Japan, as with the little men and women who inhabit it, there is something decidedly wanting; pleasant enough as a mere pastime, it begets no feeling of attachment.

On our return, when I am once more with Yves and the two mousmes climbing up the road to Diou-djen-dji, which I shall probably never see again, a vague feeling of melancholy pervades my last stroll.

It is, however, but the melancholy inseparable from all things that are about to end without possibility of return.

Moreover, this calm and splendid summer is also drawing to a close for us—since to-morrow we shall go forth to meet the autumn, in Northern China. I am beginning, alas! to count the youthful summers I may still hope for; I feel more gloomy each time another fades away, and flies to rejoin the others already disappeared in the dark and bottomless abyss, where all past things lie buried.

At midnight we return home, and my removal begins; while on board the "amazingly tall friend" kindly takes my watch.

It is a nocturnal, rapid, stealthy removal—"doyobo (thieves) fashion," remarks Yves, who in visiting the mousmes has picked up a smattering of the Nipponese language.

Messieurs the packers have, at my request, sent in the evening several charming little boxes, with compartments and false bottoms, and several paper bags (in the untearable Japanese paper), which close of themselves and are fastened by strings, also in paper, arranged beforehand in the most ingenious manner—quite the cleverest and most handy thing of its kind; for little useful trifles these people are unrivalled.

It is a real treat to pack them, and everybody lends a helping hand— Yves, Chrysantheme, Madame Prune, her daughter, and M. Sucre. By the glimmer of the reception-lamps, which are still burning, every one wraps, rolls, and ties up expeditiously, for it is already late.

Although Oyouki has a heavy heart, she can not prevent herself from indulging in a few bursts of childish laughter while she works.

Madame Prune, bathed in tears, no longer restrains her feelings; poor old lady, I really very much regret . . . .

Chrysantheme is absent-minded and silent.

But what a fearful amount of luggage! Eighteen cases or parcels, containing Buddhas, chimeras, and vases, without mentioning the last lotus that I carry away tied up in a pink cluster.

All this is piled up in the djins' carts, hired at sunset, which are waiting at the door, while their runners lie asleep on the grass.

A starlit and exquisite night. We start off with lighted lanterns, followed by the three sorrowful ladies who accompany us, and by abrupt slopes, dangerous in the darkness, we descend toward the sea.

The djins, stiffening their muscular legs, hold back with all their might the heavily loaded little cars which would run down by themselves if let alone, and that so rapidly that they would rush into empty space with my most valuable chattels. Chrysantheme walks by my side, and expresses, in a soft and winning manner, her regret that the "wonderfully tall friend" did not offer to replace me for the whole of my night-watch, as that would have allowed me to spend this last night, even till morning, under our roof.

"Listen!" she says, "come back to-morrow in the daytime, before getting under way, to bid one good-by; I shall not return to my mother until evening; you will find me still up there."

And I promise.

They stop at a certain turn, whence we have a bird's-eye view of the whole harbor. The black, stagnant waters reflect innumerable distant fires, and the ships—tiny, immovable objects, which, seen from our point of view, take the shape of fish, seem also to slumber,—little objects which serve to bear us elsewhere, to go far away, and to forget.

The three ladies are about to turn back home, for the night is already far advanced and, farther down, the cosmopolitan quarters near the quays are not safe at this unusual hour.

The moment has therefore come for Yves—who will not land again—to make his last tragic farewells to his friends the little mousmes.

I am very curious to see the parting between Yves and Chrysantheme; I listen with all my ears, I look with all my eyes, but it takes place in the simplest and quietest fashion: none of that heartbreaking which will be inevitable between Madame Prune and myself; I even notice in my mousme an indifference, an unconcern which puzzles me; I positively am at a loss to understand what it all means.

And I muse as I continue to descend toward the sea. "Her appearance of sadness was not, therefore, on Yves's account. On whose, then?" and the phrase runs through my head:

"Come back to-morrow before setting sail, to bid me goodby; I shall not return to my mother until evening; you will find me still up there."

Japan is indeed most delightful this evening, so fresh and so sweet; and little Chrysantheme was very charming just now, as she silently walked beside me through the darkness of the lane.

It is about two o'clock when we reach the 'Triomphante' in a hired sampan, where I have heaped up all my cases till there is danger of sinking. The "very tall friend" gives over to me the watch that I must keep till four o'clock; and the sailors on duty, but half awake, make a chain in the darkness, to haul on board all my fragile luggage.

CHAPTER LII

"FAREWELL!"

September 18th.

I intended to sleep late this morning, in order to make up for my lost sleep of last night.

But at eight o'clock three persons of the most extraordinary appearance, led by M. Kangourou, present themselves with profound bows at the door of my cabin. They are arrayed in long robes bedizened with dark patterns; they have the flowing locks, high foreheads, and pallid countenances of persons too exclusively devoted to the fine arts; and, perched on the top of their coiffures, they wear sailor hats of English shape tipped jauntily on one side. Tucked under their arms, they carry portfolios filled with sketches; in their hands are boxes of water-colors, pencils, and, bound together like fasces, a bundle of fine stylets with the sharp and glittering points.

At the first glance, even in the bewilderment of waking up, I gather from their appearance what their errand is, and guessing with what visitors I have to deal, I say: "Come in, Messieurs the tattooers!"

These are the specialists most in renown in Nagasaki; I had engaged them two days ago, not knowing that we were about to leave, and since they are here I will not turn them away.

My friendly and intimate relations with primitive man, in Oceania and elsewhere, have imbued me with a deplorable taste for tattoo-work; and I had wished to carry away on my own person, as a curiosity, an ornament, a specimen of the work of the Japanese tattooers, who have a delicacy of finish which is unequalled.

From their albums spread out upon my table I make my choice. There are some remarkably odd designs among them, appropriate to the different parts of the human body: emblems for the arms and legs, sprays of roses for the shoulders, great grinning faces for the middle of the back. There are even, to suit the taste of their clients who belong to foreign navies, trophies of arms, American and French flags entwined, a "God Save the Queen" amid encircling stars, and figures of women taken from Grevin's sketches in the Journal Amusant.

My choice rests upon a singular blue and pink dragon two inches long, which will have a fine effect upon my chest on the side opposite the heart.

Then follows an hour and a half of irritation and positive pain. Stretched out on my bunk and delivered over to the tender mercies of these personages, I stiffen myself and submit to the million imperceptible pricks they inflict. When by chance a little blood flows, confusing the outline by a stream of red, one of the artists hastens to stanch it with his lips, and I make no objections, knowing that this is the Japanese manner, the method used by their doctors for the wounds of both man and beast.

A piece of work, as minute and fine as that of an engraver upon stone, is slowly executed on my person; and their lean hands harrow and worry me with automatic precision.

Finally it is finished, and the tattooers, falling back with an air of satisfaction to contemplate their work, declare it to be lovely.

I dress myself quickly to go on shore, to take advantage of my last hours in Japan.

The heat is fearful to-day: the powerful September sun falls with a certain melancholy upon the yellowing leaves; it is a day of clear burning heat after an almost chilly morning.

As I did yesterday, I ascend to my lofty suburb, during the drowsy noontime, by deserted pathways filled only with light and silence.

I noiselessly open the door of my dwelling, and enter cautiously on tiptoe, for fear of Madame Prune.

At the foot of the staircase, upon the white mats, beside the little sabots and tiny sandals which are always lying about in the vestibule, a great array of luggage is ready for departure, which I recognize at a glance— pretty, dark robes, familiar to my sight, carefully folded and wrapped in blue towels tied at the four corners. I even fancy I feel a little sad when I catch sight of a corner of the famous box of letters and souvenirs peeping out of one of these bundles, in which my portrait by Ureno now reposes among divers photographs of mousmes. A sort of long-necked mandolin, also ready for departure, lies on the top of the pile in its case of figured silk. It resembles the flitting of some gipsy, or rather it reminds me of an engraving in a book of fables I owned in my childhood: the whole thing is exactly like the slender wardrobe and the long guitar which the cicala who had sung all the summer, carried upon her back when she knocked at the door of her neighbor the ant.

Poor little gipsy!

I mount the steps on tiptoe, and stop at the sound of singing that I hear in my room.

It is undoubtedly Chrysantheme's voice, and the song is quite cheerful ! This chills me and changes the current of my thoughts. I am almost sorry I have taken the trouble to come.

Mingled with the song is a noise I can not understand: Chink! chink! a clear metallic ring as of coins flung vigorously on the floor. I am well aware that this vibrating house exaggerates every sound during the silence of night; but all the same, I am puzzled to know what my mousme can be doing. Chink! chink! is she amusing herself with quoits, or the 'jeu du crapaud', or pitch-and-toss?

Nothing of the kind! I fancy I have guessed, and I continue my upward progress still more gently, on all fours, with the precautions of a red Indian, to give myself for the last time the pleasure of surprising her.

She has not heard me come in. In our great white room, emptied and swept out, where the clear sunshine pours in, and the soft wind, and the yellowed leaves of the garden, she is sitting all alone, her back turned to the door; she is dressed for walking, ready to go to her mother's, her rose-colored parasol beside her.

On the floor are spread out all the fine silver dollars which, according to our agreement, I had given her the evening before. With the competent dexterity of an old money-changer she fingers them, turns them over, throws them on the floor, and, armed with a little mallet ad hoc, rings them vigorously against her ear, singing the while I know not what little pensive bird-like song which I daresay she improvises as she goes along.

Well, after all, it is even more completely Japanese than I could possibly have imagined it—this last scene of my married life! I feel inclined to laugh. How simple I have been, to allow myself to be taken in by the few clever words she whispered yesterday, as she walked beside me, by a tolerably pretty little phrase embellished as it was by the silence of two o'clock in the morning, and all the wonderful enchantments of night.

Ah! not more for Yves than for me, not more for me than for Yves, has any feeling passed through that little brain, that little heart.

When I have looked at her long enough, I call:

"Hi! Chrysantheme!"

She turns confused, and reddening even to her ears at having been caught at this work.

She is quite wrong, however, to be so much troubled, for I am, on the contrary, delighted. The fear that I might be leaving her in some sadness had almost given me a pang, and I infinitely prefer that this marriage should end as it had begun, in a joke.

"That is a good idea of yours," I say; "a precaution which should always be taken in this country of yours, where so many evil-minded people are clever in forging money. Make haste and get through it before I start, and if any false pieces have found their way into the number, I will willingly replace them."

However, she refuses to continue before me, and I expected as much; to do so would have been contrary to all her notions of politeness, hereditary and acquired, all her conventionality, all her Japanesery. With a disdainful little foot, clothed as usual in exquisite socks, with a special hood for the great toe, she pushes away the piles of white dollars and scatters them on the mats.

"We have hired a large, covered sampan," she says to change the conversation, "and we are all going together—Campanule, Jonquille, Touki, all your mousmes—to watch your vessel set sail. Pray sit down and stay a few minutes."

"No, I really can not stay. I have several things to do in the town, you see, and the order was given for every one to be on board by three o'clock in time for muster before starting. Moreover, I would prefer to escape, as you can imagine, while Madame Prune is still enjoying her siesta; I should be afraid of being drawn into some corner, or of provoking some heartrending parting scene."

Chrysantheme bows her head and says no more, but seeing that I am really going, rises to escort me.

Without speaking, without the slightest noise, she follows me as we descend the staircase and cross the garden full of sunshine, where the dwarf shrubs and the deformed flowers seem, like the rest of the household, plunged in warm somnolence.

At the outer gate I stop for the last adieu: the little sad pout has reappeared, more accentuated than ever, on Chrysantheme's face; it is the right thing, it is correct, and I should feel offended now were it absent.

Well, little mousme, let us part good friends; one last kiss even, if you like. I took you to amuse me; you have not perhaps succeeded very well, but after all you have done what you could: given me your little face, your little curtseys, your little music; in short, you have been pleasant enough in your Japanese way. And who knows, perchance I may yet think of you sometimes when I recall this glorious summer, these pretty, quaint gardens, and the ceaseless concert of the cicalas.

She prostrates herself on the threshold of the door, her forehead against the ground, and remains in this attitude of superlatively polite salute as long as I am in sight, while I go down the pathway by which I am to disappear for ever.

As the distance between us increases, I turn once or twice to look at her again; but it is a mere civility, and meant to return as it deserves her grand final salutation.

CHAPTER LIII

OFF FOR CHINA

When I entered the town, at the turn of the principal street, I had the good luck to meet Number 415, my poor relative. I was just at that moment in want of a speedy djin, and I at once got into his vehicle; besides, it was an alleviation to my feelings, in this hour of departure, to take my last drive in company with a member of my family.

Unaccustomed as I was to be out of doors during the hours of siesta, I had never yet seen the streets of the town thus overwhelmed by the sunshine, thus deserted in the silence and solitary brilliancy peculiar to all hot countries.

In front of all the shops hang white shades, adorned here and there with slight designs in black, in the quaintness of which lurks I know not what—something mysterious: dragons, emblems, symbolical figures. The sky is too glaring; the light crude, implacable; never has this old town of Nagasaki appeared to me so old, so worm-eaten, so bald, notwithstanding all its veneer of new papers and gaudy paintings. These little wooden houses, of such marvellous cleanly whiteness inside, are black outside, timeworn, disjointed and grimacing. When one looks closely, this grimace is to be found everywhere: in the hideous masks laughing in the shop-fronts of the innumerable curio-shops; in the grotesque figures, the playthings, the idols, cruel, suspicious, mad; it is even found in the buildings: in the friezes of the religious porticoes, in the roofs of the thousand pagodas, of which the angles and cable-ends writhe and twist like the yet dangerous remains of ancient and malignant beasts.

And the disturbing intensity of expression reigning over inanimate nature, contrasts with the almost absolute blank of the human countenance, with the smiling foolishness of the simple little folk who meet one's gaze, as they patiently carry on their minute trades in the gloom of their tiny open-fronted houses. Workmen squatted on their heels, carving with their imperceptible tools the droll or odiously obscene ivory ornaments, marvellous cabinet curiosities which have made Japan so famous with the European amateurs who have never seen it. Unconscious artists tracing with steady hand on a background of lacquer or of porcelain traditional designs learned by heart, or transmitted to their brains by a process of heredity through thousands of years; automatic painters, whose storks are similar to those of M. Sucre, with the inevitable little rocks, or little butterflies eternally the same. The least of these illuminators, with his insignificant, eyeless face, possesses at his fingers' ends the maximum of dexterity in this art of decoration, light and wittily incongruous, which threatens to invade us in France, in this epoch of imitative decadence, and which has become the great resource of our manufacturers of cheap "objects of art."

Is it because I am about to leave this country, because I have no longer any link to bind me to it, any resting-place on its soil, that my spirit is ready on the wing? I know not, but it seems to me I have never as clearly seen and comprehended it as to-day. And more even than ever do I find it little, aged, with worn-out blood and worn-out sap; I feel more fully its antediluvian antiquity, its centuries of mummification, which will soon degenerate into hopeless and grotesque buffoonery, as it comes into contact with Western novelties.

It is getting late; little by little, the siestas are everywhere coming to an end; the queer little streets brighten up and begin to swarm in the sunshine with many-colored parasols. Now begins the procession of ugliness of the most impossible description—a procession of long-robed, grotesque figures capped with pot-hats or sailors' headgear. Business transactions begin again, and the struggle for existence, close and bitter here as in one of our own artisan quarters, but meaner and smaller.

At the moment of my departure, I find within myself only a smile of careless mockery for the swarming crowd of this Lilliputian curtseying people—laborious, industrious, greedy of gain, tainted with a constitutional affectation, hereditary insignificance, and incurable monkeyishness.

Poor cousin Number 415! how right I was to have held him in good esteem! He was by far the best and most disinterested of my Japanese family. When all my commissions are finished, he puts up his little vehicle under a tree, and, much touched by my departure, insists upon escorting me on board the 'Triomphante', to watch over my final purchases in the sampan which conveys me to the ship, and to see them himself safely into my cabin.

His, indeed, is the only hand I clasp with a really friendly feeling, without a suppressed smile, on quitting Japan.

No doubt in this country, as in many others, there is more honest friendship and less ugliness among the simple beings devoted to purely physical work.

At five o'clock in the afternoon we set sail.

Along the line of the shore are two or three sampans; in them the mousmes, shut up in the narrow cabins, peep at us through the tiny windows, half hiding their faces on account of the sailors; these are our wives, who have wished, out of politeness, to look upon us once more.

There are other sampans as well, in which other Japanese women are also watching our departure. These stand upright, under great parasols decorated with big black letters and daubed over with clouds of varied and startling colors.

CHAPTER LIV

A FADING PICTURE

We move slowly out of the wide green bay. The groups of women grow smaller in the distance. The country of round umbrellas with a thousand ribs fades gradually from our sight.

Now the vast ocean opens before us, immense, colorless, solitary; a solemn repose after so much that is too ingenious and too small.

The wooded mountains, the flowery capes disappear. And Japan remains faithful to itself, with its picturesque rocks, its quaint islands on which the trees tastefully arrange themselves in groups—studied, perhaps, but charmingly pretty.

CHAPTER LV

A WITHERED LOTUS-FLOWER

One evening, in my cabin, in the midst of the Yellow Sea, my eyes fall upon the lotus-blossoms brought from Diou-djen-dji; they had lasted several days; but now they are withered, and strew my carpet pathetically with their pale pink petals.

I, who have carefully kept so many faded flowers, fallen, alas! into dust, stolen here and there, at moments of parting in different parts of the world; I, who have kept so many that the collection is now an absurd, an indistinguishable herbarium—I try hard, but without success, to awaken some sentiment for these lotus—and yet they are the last living souvenirs of my summer at Nagasaki.

I pick them up, however, with a certain amount of consideration, and I open my port-hole.

From the gray misty sky a strange light falls upon the waters; a dim and gloomy twilight descends, yellowish upon this Yellow Sea. We feel that we are moving northward, that autumn is approaching.

I throw the poor lotus into the boundless waste of waters, making them my best excuses for consigning them, natives of Japan, to a grave so solemn and so vast.

LVI

An Appeal to the Gods

*Ô Ama-Terace-Omi-Kami, wash me clean
from this little marriage of mine,
in the waters of the river of Kamo !*

THE END

Annex

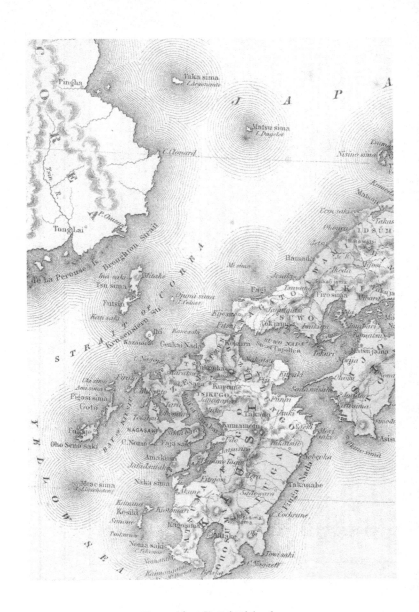

Nagasaki on Kyūshū island.

View from Nagasaki.

Made in the USA
Monee, IL
27 August 2022